Face to Face with a Nightmare

It loomed up in front of him, surprising him even though he was prepared. It was a huge shape with fur and teeth and yellow eyes. The creature saw him at the same time and they both reacted. The wolf rose up and roared at him, took a swipe at him with one huge paw. Clint fired his gun twice, was sure he hit the thing, but it turned and ran off.

He chased it, and then realized he had been clawed . . .

THE GUNSMITH

381

BLOOD TRAIL

J. R. ROBERTS

JOVE BOOKS, NEW YORK

THE BERKLEY PUBLISHING GROUP
Published by the Penguin Group
Penguin Group (USA)
375 Hudson Street, New York, New York 10014, USA

USA | Canada | UK | Ireland | Australia | New Zealand | India | South Africa | China

Penguin Books Ltd., Registered Offices: 80 Strand, London WC2R 0RL, England
For more information about the Penguin Group, visit penguin.com.

BLOOD TRAIL

A Jove Book / published by arrangement with the author

Jove Books are published by The Berkley Publishing Group.
JOVE® is a registered trademark of Penguin Group (USA).
The "J" design is a trademark of Penguin Group (USA).

For information, address: The Berkley Publishing Group,
a division of Penguin Group (USA),
375 Hudson Street, New York, New York 10014.

ISBN: 978-0-515-15389-7

PUBLISHING HISTORY
Jove mass-market edition / September 2013

PRINTED IN THE UNITED STATES OF AMERICA

10 9 8 7 6 5 4 3 2 1

Cover illustration by Sergio Giovine.

ONE

Frederick Talbot climbed into the back of his wagon and closed the flap. Around him he could hear the others in the wagon train conversing beside their fires, trading stories, or offering parting words as they turned in for the night. He could also hear Captain Sean Parker giving orders for when they would rise and start out again.

The days of the wagon trains made up of a hundred prairie schooners heading west were gone. This was a train of ten wagons, a group of neighbors from the East who had decided to move out West and were traveling together for safety's sake.

Despite their small size, they had elected officers, and had hired a guide and a man to be captain. In some respects, this might also have been considered the last wagon train. At least, that was how Captain Parker thought of it.

But tonight Frederick's thoughts were elsewhere, not on the history of the wagon trains, or their start time in the morning.

He went to a cedar chest he kept hidden beneath a blanket, unlocked it with a key, and opened it. From inside he withdrew a small wooden box, also locked. He took out a smaller key, unlocked it, and opened it. The items inside were those he had hoped never to need, but there they were.

There was a set of rosary beads, a crucifix, a prayer book, a pistol, a silver bullet mold, a wooden mallet, three sharpened wooden stakes, some garlic paste, and vials of holy water, all lying in felt in the oak wood box.

This was his vampire kit.

Frederick had come to the United States from Germany. His neighbors had come from Germany, Poland, and Romania. They had thought to settle in the East, but did not encounter the open arms they had hoped for, so they decided to go west.

Frederick Talbot carried this kit with him wherever he went, and he knew many of the others did, too. Some of them claimed not to believe in vampires and werewolves now that they were in the United States, but Talbot was not yet ready to give up that part of his heritage.

He touched the mallet, the stakes, picked up a vial of the holy water to study it and then return it to its felt bed. Finally, he closed the box, locked it, and placed it back in the chest.

"Papa?" his daughter's voice came from outside. "Papa, what are you doing?"

"Nothing," he called back, hastily turning the key on the chest and then covering it with the blanket. "I will be right out."

He moved to the back of the wagon and pushed the flap aside.

"Papa, supper is ready," his seventeen-year-old-daughter, Sarah, said. "Come to the fire."

"I am coming," he said, stepping down from the wagon.

"Careful," she said, "do not break your neck." She reached out to help him.

"Do not fuss," he said, slapping her hand away. Sarah had been born to Frederick and his late wife, Delilah, late in life. So Talbot was, at sixty-six years of age, the father of a healthy seventeen-year-old daughter. Healthy in that the boys on the wagon train were all mooning over her, whether they were teenagers or older.

Talbot followed his daughter to the fire, where some of their neighbors had gathered. The Talbot family usually ate together with the Gerhardt and Mueller families.

Sarah spooned out a good portion of stew into a wooden bowl and handed it to her father.

"What were you doing in your wagon, Frederick?" his longtime friend, Howard Gerhardt, asked him. They had come to the United States on the same ship back when both of their children were young.

"Nothing."

In a low tone Howard asked, "Were you looking at that vampire kit again?"

"Shhh," Talbot urged him.

"You are a silly man, my friend," Howard said. "The old ways have not followed us here."

"You do not know that," Talbot said. "It is better to be safe."

"Even if they have followed us," Gerhardt said, "we have certainly left them behind in Pennsylvania."

"I am not convinced," Talbot said, "and I have a daughter to protect."

"And I have a son," Gerhardt reminded him.

"Boys can fend for themselves," Talbot said. "It is my job to protect my daughter until she finds a husband."

Gerhardt looked across the fire to where Talbot's lovely daughter, Sarah, was handing his son, Carl, a bowl of stew.

"Perhaps she has already found a candidate."

Talbot did not reply. Gerhardt was his good friend, but he did not think Carl was a suitable match for his daughter. And therefore, he kept his mouth full of stew so he could not reply.

TWO

Clint Adams was in Effingham, Missouri, for three days when there was a murder . . .

On his first day he met Rita St. John, who ran a dress shop on Main Street. He'd actually been walking past the store, on the way to find a restaurant, when she came out the door and they collided.

"Oh, I'm so sorry," she said. "I wasn't looking—"

"No, no," he insisted, "it was my fault. Are you all right?"

"Oh, yes," she said. "I was just—I don't have much business today, so I was going to close early."

She was a tall redhead in her late thirties, with short hair and green eyes, a lovely face despite a nose that might have been a bit too big, if a man wanted to be critical. Clint didn't. The attraction was immediate.

"Well," he said, "I just got to town and was trying to find a decent place to eat. Do you know of one?"

"Sure," she said. "There are several good places in town. What are you looking for?"

"A good steak."

"Then you have to go to Andy's Café. It's a few blocks that way, and you turn—"

"You wouldn't be hungry, would you?"

She stopped short.

"Hungry? Well, I, uh, I could eat—"

"Why don't you take me to Andy's," he said, "and then I'll repay the favor by buying you a meal. We can call it a late lunch."

"Well . . . I, uh, don't know you—"

"My name is Clint Adams," he said. "I'm in town to visit my friend Ray Bullet."

"Ray? Why, he's the sheriff."

"Yes, I know."

"Well," she said after a moment, "if you're friends with the sheriff, I guess it's all right. Just let me lock up."

He waited while she locked the front door of the shop and put the key away in her small bag.

"My name is Rita St. John. Andy's is this way," she said.

"Just lead the way, Rita . . ."

They ate together, exchanged histories. She had been in Effingham for five years, trying to get her business going. He never did find out that first day if she recognized his name. But their attraction was so strong that she ended up in his hotel room with him, and he never did get to see Ray Bullet that first day either . . .

He woke the next morning with Rita beside him. They had been together for over fifteen hours since their first meeting, much of them spent in bed.

She was a tall, full-bodied woman with pear-shaped breasts topped by brown nipples, and a tangle of copper-colored hair between her long legs.

She woke while he was staring at her admiringly, and covered her face with her hands.

"Oh, my God," she said.

"What?"

She peered at him from between slightly spread fingers.

"I've never done this before."

"What? Had sex? I thought you seemed at least a little experienced."

"No, not that," she said. "I've had sex before, but never with a man I don't know."

"I thought we got to know each other very well over a couple of good steaks."

"And after a few hours we ended up back here," she said. She dropped her hands and looked around. "What time is it?"

"It's early morning."

"Morning?" she asked. "You mean as in, the next day?"

"Yes," he said, "it's the next day. Technically speaking, we have now known each other for two days."

"Oh, God," she said, again covering her face.

"Was it that bad?"

She dropped her hands again and looked at him.

"No, no," she said, "it was wonderful. I mean, it was very . . . I'm just not used to . . ."

He rolled toward her, put his hand on her belly, which twitched.

"So I guess you don't want me to do this," he said, then lowered his hand, "or this," he moved his middle finger, "or this."

"Oh!" she said, jumping. "Oh, yes, please, do that some more."

She put her hands at her sides and arched her back as he moved his middle finger just a little, just lightly touching her.

He leaned over to kiss her right breast, then her left. They were heavy, leaning to the side just a bit beneath their own weight. Her nipples were large, and he licked and sucked them as he continued to stroke her with his finger.

"Oh, God," she said, grabbing for his head. He got away from her, though, and kissed his way down over her belly until he could replace the tip of his finger with the tip of his tongue. He licked her until her entire body went taut and she spasmed beneath him, gathering the sheet in her fists and biting her lip so she wouldn't scream . . .

At that moment there was a knock on the door. She grabbed the sheet and covered herself with it, as if the person at the door could see her.

"Relax," he said, "they can't see you."

"What if it's someone I know?" she whispered.

"The only person who knows I was coming to town is Ray Bullet."

"Oh, God. Ray?" she said. "He can't find me here."

The knocking persisted.

"Well," he said, "let me see if it's him, and then I'll make sure he doesn't see you. How's that?"

"Okay."

He got to his feet, pulled on his pants, and grabbed his gun.

"Do you need that to answer the door?" she asked.

"Always."

He went to the door with the gun in his right hand, used his left to turn the knob and open it a crack. Ray Bullet stood in the hall.

"Clint."

"Ray," he said. "Look, I'm sorry I didn't come see you when I got in, but—"

"Never mind that," Bullet said. "Get dressed. I need you."

"Need me for what?"

"I don't have a deputy, and I have a problem."

"What kind of problem?"

"The worst kind," Sheriff Ray Bullet said. "There's been a murder."

THREE

The body was a bloody mess.

It had been found in a clearing near town by two young boys who were supposed to be in school. Horrified, they had run to school and told their teacher what they'd found.

"What the hell did this?" Ray Bullet said.

"I don't know."

The body had been eviscerated, blood spread out everywhere. Clint got closer, crouched down to take a good look.

"It looks like he got his throat ripped out," he said. "Maybe that was first, and the feast came later."

"You ever see a wolf do this?" Bullet asked.

"No," Clint said, "I've seen cleaner kills by wolves. But maybe a wolf did it, and some other animals came by later and did the rest."

"Only one problem," Bullet said.

"What's that?"

"There haven't been any wolves around here in a long time."

"Well," Clint said, "maybe you've got one now."

Clint stood up.

"We should go back to town and get somebody out here

to clean this up," Bullet said. "We don't want anybody else seein' it."

Ray Bullet was in his early fifties, with steel gray hair and face that looked chiseled out of rock. He was tall and broad-shouldered, his physique showing no signs of aging. He still stood a good six-foot-three.

"Wait," Clint said.

He walked around the area a few minutes, checking the ground, looking for sign of man or beast.

"See anything?" Bullet asked.

Clint came back to the body, was about to say that he saw nothing when he spotted something.

"Look."

"What?" Bullet asked.

"There. In the blood."

Bullet squinted.

"What is that? A boot print?"

"Sure looks like one," Clint said. "But . . . only one?"

"Why aren't there bloody tracks leading away?" Bullet asked.

"I don't know," Clint said. "Is there anybody in town who can read sign?"

"I thought you were reading it."

"We need somebody who can read it better than I can," Clint told him.

"Lemme think," Bullet said. "Like I said, we ain't had any wolves around here in a while, so we haven't needed any hunters."

"Then I suggest we move this body, but we don't clean the area up," Clint said. "Not yet anyway. Not until we can find somebody to read the sign."

"Okay."

"We need somebody to pick up the body without trampling all over the area," Clint said.

"I can talk to the undertaker," Bullet said. "He can have his men come out, and they'll be careful."

"You better be here to make sure they're careful."

"No," Bullet said, "we've got to start looking for whoever did this."

"We?" Clint asked. "How did I get roped into this problem?"

"I told you," Bullet said. "I don't have a deputy. I need you."

"Ray—"

"Clint."

"Let's just get back to town," Clint said. "We can talk about it later."

"Okay," Bullet said. "Okay."

With a last look at the destroyed body, they turned and headed back.

FOUR

Clint sat in front of the sheriff's desk, drinking coffee from a chipped white mug. The sheriff poured himself a cup and sat behind the desk.

"Okay," he said. "The undertaker's gonna be real careful about moving the body. He'll try not to disturb the surrounding area too much."

"What about a tracker?"

"Nothing yet," Bullet said.

"So where do you want to start?"

"I can't see that the murderer is anybody from this town," Bullet said.

"Do we know who the victim is?"

"No."

"Then how can you say that?"

"These are good people, Clint," Bullet said. "I can't see anyone from this town killin' somebody that way."

"It looked to me like there was a lot of anger involved, Ray," Clint said. "That, or a lot of passion."

"I'm thinkin' a stranger."

"Any strangers in town?"

"Strictly speakin'," Bullet said. "One."

"Who's that?"

"You."

"Nobody else has ridden into town?"

"Not in the past few days," Bullet said, "except . . ."

"Except what?"

"There's a wagon train camped right outside of town," Bullet said.

"Wagon train?" Clint said. "There are no more wagon trains, Ray."

"Not like there used to be," Bullet said, "but this is a bunch of folks traveling from east to west together in wagons. What would you call it?"

"Yeah, okay," Clint said. "How many wagons are we talking about?"

"About ten, I think."

"Have you been out there?"

"No," he said, "but they've been here in town, buying supplies."

"What kind of people are they?"

"Foreign," Bullet said.

"From where?"

"Europe," Bullet said. "Germany, I think. Poland. Some other countries I've never heard of."

"Okay," Clint said, "so I suppose we should go out and talk to them."

"That's the plan."

"But we should go to the undertaker's first."

"For what?"

"To look at the body once he has it cleaned up," Clint said. "And to look at the victim's clothes."

"His clothes?"

"Might give us an idea of where he's from," Clint said. "Or if he's local."

"Well," Bullet said, "I couldn't tell from lookin' at him if he was local or not. Too much blood coverin' his face."

"All the more reason for us to look at him when he's cleaned up."

"Yeah, okay," Clint said. "Exactly when do you want to do that?"

"The sooner the better," Bullet said. He took a bottle of whiskey from his drawer and poured some into their cups. "As soon as we finish our coffee."

FIVE

Clint and Bullet entered the undertaker's office.

"Afternoon, Sheriff," a tall, slender man said. Not painfully thin, as undertakers were expected to be, and not as old as Clint had expected. This man seemed to be in his thirties, and looked more like a doctor or a lawyer than an undertaker.

"The body here, Zeke?" Bullet asked.

"In the back," the undertaker, Zeke Taylor, said. "The doc is with him."

"The doctor?" Clint asked. "What for? He's dead, isn't he?"

"The doctor was curious about the way the man died," Taylor said. "He asked to be allowed to examine the body. I didn't think you'd mind, Sheriff."

"I don't," Bullet said. He looked at Clint. "We can use his comments." He looked back at Taylor. "Did you clean him up?"

"I did."

"His face?"

"Washed it clean."

"Do you know him, Zeke?" Bullet asked. "Is he from town?"

"Never saw him before, Ray."

"Where are his clothes?" Clint asked.

"In the corner of the same room."

"Anything in his pockets?"

"I didn't go through the pockets," the man said. "I left that for the sheriff."

"All right, Zeke," the sheriff said. "Can we see the body?"

"Right back here."

Taylor led them to a curtain, swept it aside, and let them enter, then closed the curtain in case someone should enter the establishment.

The body was laid out on a table, and hovering over it was a man who looked more like an undertaker than a doctor. In his fifties, he was tall, painfully thin, with hollowed-out eyes and cheeks.

"Doc," Bullet said.

"Sheriff."

"This is Clint Adams."

"Pleased to meet you," the doctor said.

"Clint, Doc Miller."

Clint nodded.

"What can you tell me, Doc?" Bullet asked.

The doctor's hands were bloody as he pointed with his little finger.

"Looks to me like his throat was torn out first, and then they went to work on his torso. They tore open his chest and his belly. Some of his organs are missing."

"They took them away?" Bullet asked.

"Or ate them," the doc said.

"All right," Bullet said, "let us have a look, will you?"

"He's been cleaned up," Doc said, "but it's still not pretty."

He stepped aside, stood next to the undertaker. Clint was struck by the contrast between the two men, whose physical appearances seemed to fit the other's occupation.

The body was naked, the face scrubbed clean, the rest of him still somewhat bloody. The ravaged chest and belly had been spread open even more for examination. Clint had seen a lot of things in his time, but never that.

Despite the fact that the throat had been torn out, his face seemed serene in death.

"You know him, Doc?" Bullet asked.

"Never saw him."

"Me neither," Bullet said. "Clint?"

"Not me."

"Ever see anythin' like this before in an animal attack?"

"No," Clint said. "And I've seen wolf kills, cat kills, bears . . . nothing like this."

"Doc," Bullet said, "that throat wound. That would've killed him, right?"

"Oh, yes," the doctor said. "The other wounds would have been postmortem."

"Huh?" Bullet said.

"After death," the doctor said.

"Oh."

"Where are the clothes?" Clint asked.

The undertaker pointed to a wadded-up bundle in a corner. Clint walked over, tried to spread the bloody clothes out without getting too much blood on him.

"Pockets?" Bullet asked, looking over his shoulder.

Clint prodded the trousers and said, "They seem to be empty."

"Clothes don't look store bought," Sheriff Bullet said.

"That's what I thought, too," the undertaker commented.

"Yes," Clint said, looking closely, "the sewing looks homemade."

"Not a man with money, then," Bullet said. "Robbery is probably out of the question."

"Looks young," the doc said.

They all turned and looked at him. He was once again peering at the body.

"Might even have been under twenty."

They all walked back to the table.

"He's right," Clint said. "This is a kid."

"Was," Taylor said.

"What?" Bullet asked.

"The deceased," the undertaker said. "We say 'was,' not 'is.'"

Clint ignored him.

"Who would want to kill this kid in this way?" he wondered aloud.

"Someone angry," the doctor said.

Clint looked at Bullet.

"We better ride out and talk to those people."

"The wagon train?" the doc asked.

"Yes," Bullet said.

"Why them?"

"They're strangers," Bullet said. "The only strangers in town."

"They seem like nice people," Doc Miller said.

"What kind of contact have you had with them?" Clint asked.

"A few of them brought their kids in to see me," Miller said.

"They sick?" Bullet asked.

"A couple of colds," Miller said. "One broken arm. That's about it."

"What do you know about them?" Clint asked.

"Very old world," Miller said, "looking for a new one."

"German? Polish, like the sheriff says?" Clint asked.

"Romanian, too."

"Where's that?" Bullet asked. "Roman-y-what?"

"Romania," Miller said. "Not sure where it is."

"Well," Bullet said, "we better get out there."

"Do they speak English?" Clint asked Miller.

"Most of them," the doc said.

"Don't worry," Bullet said, "their captain and their guide are Americans."

"They're nice people, Sheriff," the doctor said.

"Nice people kill, too, Doc," Sheriff Bullet said. "I've seen it too many times."

SIX

"Riders!"

Talbot and Gerhardt looked up from what they were doing to see the two riders approaching.

"Who are they?" Talbot asked.

"Looks like they're from town," Captain Parker said.

"I think I see a badge," Dave Barrett, the guide, said.

"Ah," Parker said, "the sheriff."

"What can he want?" Abel Zonofsky asked.

"Well," Parker said, "sometimes the town sheriff suspects strangers of petty thefts that take place in town." He turned and looked at the assembled members of the train. "If anyone took anything while they were in town, now's the time to tell us."

"We are not thieves," Gerhardt said.

Parker looked around.

"So say you all?"

They all nodded, men, women, and children alike.

"All right, then," Parker said, "just let me do the talking."

"That's Parker," Bullet said as they approached. "He's the captain."

"Of a ten-wagon train?" Clint asked.

"And they have a guide."

"Well, that makes sense."

"Fella's name is Barrett."

"Don't know him."

"What about Parker?" Bullet asked. "Captain Sean Parker?"

"Him neither."

"Okay."

By the time they reached the camp, the people had all gathered around.

"Captain," Bullet said, reining in.

"Sheriff."

"This is my friend, Clint Adams. He's my . . . acting deputy."

"I know Mr. Adams's reputation," Parker said. "What brings you out here?"

"Murder, I'm afraid," Bullet said.

"Murder? Who?"

"We're not sure yet," Bullet said. "We found a man just outside of town who had been murdered in a way that made it impossible to identify him."

"All right," Parker said. "But why come to us?"

"Well," the sheriff said, "first to see if any of your party is missing."

Parker looked around.

"Anyone missing?" he asked.

Everybody exchanged glances and looked around, then looked back at Parker.

Parker turned back to Bullet.

"No one is missing," he said. "What else?"

"Has anyone been away from camp for an extended period of time since last night?"

"No," Parker said.

"You don't have to ask?"

"No."

"Well," Bullet said, "let me tell you that the man who was killed was . . . ripped apart, as if by a wolf, or some other animal."

That got a rise out of the assembled people. The woman grabbed their children and held them close.

"Ripped apart?" Talbot asked.

"That's right."

Talbot stepped forward.

"As if by a wolf?"

"Yes," Bullet said.

"Was . . . was the throat ripped out?" Talbot asked.

"Yeah, it was," Bullet said. He frowned. "Who are you, sir?"

"This is Mr. Talbot," Parker said.

"Well, Mr. Talbot," Bullet said, "what would you know about this?"

"I know nothing about it," Talbot said, "but I believe I might be able to help."

"How?" Clint asked. "How could you help?"

"I am a hunter."

"Can you track?" Clint asked.

"Indeed I can."

Clint looked at Bullet and raised his eyebrows.

"Sir," Bullet said, "do you have a horse?"

"Yes, I do."

"Would you come along with us and take a look at the scene?"

"And the body?" Clint asked.

"Yes," Talbot said. "Let me saddle my horse."

Clint and Bullet remained mounted and waited, while the assembled crowd stared at them.

"Papa," Sarah said as her father saddled his horse, "what are you doing?"

"I am trying to be helpful, child."

"But this is not for you to do."

"I am a hunter," he reminded her.

"Yes," she said, "but you did not tell the men what you hunt."

"They did not ask."

"And if they do?"

"I will tell them."

"They will think you are crazy," she said. "The men in this country do not understand."

Talbot turned to his daughter and said, "Perhaps this body will make them understand."

"Papa—"

"I have to go, child," he said. "You stay close to the wagon, do you hear?"

"I hear you, Papa," she said. "Please be careful."

"I will."

"I mean," she said, "be careful of what you say to these men."

He put his hand on his daughter's shoulders, then walked away with his horse.

Clint saw the man approaching them, leading a worn, old mare.

"That's a horse?" Bullet said, aloud.

Talbot heard him.

"She is a fine animal," he said. "I have had her a long time."

"Can she keep up?" Bullet asked.

Talbot mounted up.

"Do not worry," he said, "she will keep up."

"You want me to come along, Sheriff?" Parker asked.

"I think you'd better stay close to your people, Captain," Bullet said. "Don't worry, we'll bring Mr. Talbot back to you."

Talbot's daughter came and stood next to the captain.

The older man put his arm around her, which did not please Talbot one bit.

"Sarah," he said, "stay close to the wagon."

"Yes, Papa."

He looked at Bullet and Clint.

"Shall we go?"

SEVEN

Clint and Bullet led Frederick Talbot to the place where the body had been found. The blood had soaked into the ground. There was a clean space in the middle, where the body had been removed.

"There you go," Bullet said. "Have a look."

Frederick Talbot dismounted and walked over to the spot. He crouched down, reached out with his hand, but didn't actually touch the ground.

"I see one boot print," Talbot said.

"Yeah," Bullet said, "we saw that. But why aren't there more?"

Talbot stood up, started to walk around.

"Here!" he said.

Clint and Bullet dismounted and walked over to where Talbot was standing.

"Where?" Bullet asked.

"Look close."

Clint was looking for an imprint in the ground. But he saw what Talbot was pointing at. It was a footprint in blood. And it was from an animal.

"I see it," he said.

"Where?" Bullet asked anxiously.

"There," Talbot said, crouching down and pointing. "Right there."

"What kind of track is that?" he asked, squinting. "A wolf?"

"If it is," Clint said, "it's a big one."

"A really big one," Bullet said.

Clint looked at Talbot.

"What about it? A wolf?"

"Could be," Talbot said.

Clint had the feeling the man was holding something back.

"I'll look for more," Talbot said, and walked off.

"What the hell—" Bullet said, staring at the print.

"He knows more than what he's saying," Clint commented.

"Like what?"

"I don't know."

"Think he knows who the killer is?"

"I don't know," Clint said. "It's just . . . something."

"Let's ask 'im," Bullet said.

"Let's wait 'til he's finished," Clint said. "See what he tells us."

"Okay," Bullet said, "but keep an eye on him."

They watched and waited while Talbot studied the entire area in a twenty-foot radius. Finally, he came back to them.

"I see two sets of tracks," he said, "man and beast."

"So there was a man," Bullet said, "with the animal?"

"The man might have been your victim," Talbot said. "I suggest you check the bottoms of his boots for blood."

"What else did you find?" Clint asked.

"I have told you—"

"No," Clint said, "there's something else."

Talbot studied the two of them, then said, "All right. Come with me."

They followed him until they were about twenty-five feet away.

"There." He pointed.

"What the hell—" Clint said.

"What is it?" Bullet asked. "Why can't I see what you fellas see?"

Clint leaned over and pointed, saying, "There."

Bullet saw another footprint, that of a man, in blood. Only this one was . . . a bare foot.

EIGHT

They rode back to town, taking Frederick Talbot with them. First they stopped at the undertaker's.

"More questions?" Zeke Taylor asked.

"We just need to look at the soles of the victim's boots," Bullet said, "and his feet."

"Feet?"

"Bare feet," Clint said.

"All right," Taylor said. "He and his clothes are still where they were before."

They went into the back, taking Talbot with them. While they examined the boots, and the bottoms of the man's feet, Talbot studied the body.

"Blood on his boots," Bullet said.

"But none on his bare feet," Clint said. "Plus, the bare footprint we saw was larger than his foot."

Clint and Bullet turned to Talbot.

"What do you see, Mr. Talbot?" Clint asked. "Have you seen anything like this before?"

Talbot turned to them and stared. For a moment Clint thought he wasn't going to answer.

"I have seen this," Talbot said, "in my country."

"What country is that?" Clint asked.

"Romania."

"Okay," Bullet said, "let's go to my office and talk."

At the sheriff's office, Bullet made coffee, and when they all had a cup, they sat down to talk.

"All right, Mr. Talbot," Bullet said. "When you saw this in your country . . . what were the circumstances?"

Talbot didn't answer right away.

"What did this?" Clint asked. "In your country, I mean."

"It was . . . a wolf."

"A wolf?" Clint asked. "With a print that big?"

"It was not . . . a normal wolf."

"You have abnormal wolves in your country?" Bullet asked.

"Yes," Talbot said. "Bigger. Different."

"Well," Bullet said, "that may be, but we don't have those kinds of wolves in this country."

Talbot shrugged and said, "I am only telling you what I saw."

Clint and Bullet exchanged a glance, and then Clint asked, "Tell me something, Mr. Talbot."

"Yes?"

"Can you track this thing?"

"The animal?" Talbot asked. "Or the man?"

"Both," Bullet said.

"I could," the man said, "but . . ."

"But what?"

"I must travel with the others," Talbot said. "My daughter . . ."

"Don't worry," Clint said. "After you track it, and we catch it, we can get you back to the wagons. Back to your daughter."

"You do not understand," Talbot said. "I cannot leave my daughter there alone. She needs me to be there to protect her."

"But she's not alone," the sheriff said. "There are other people there. And the captain."

Talbot shook his head and said, "The captain is in charge there . . . and he is the one I need to protect my daughter from."

NINE

Sarah saw the flap of her wagon open and then Captain Sean Parker stuck his head inside.

"You gonna stay in there all night?" he asked.

"I promised my father," she said, "I would stay with the wagon until he returned."

"Well," the older man said, "okay. I could come in there with you."

"No!" Sarah said. "That will not be necessary. I—I will be fine."

"Aw, come on, Sarah," Parker said. He leaned in so he could touch the smooth skin of her arm. "I just want to be nice to you. I want to keep you safe."

She pulled her arm away and said, "I appreciate that, I really do."

Parker grinned and was about to climb into her wagon when someone said from behind him, "Don't do that!"

Sarah knew the voice. It was young Carl Gerhardt, who she knew was in love with her. He reminded her of Vlad, the boy she'd left behind at home in Romania. He loved her, too.

Captain Parker paused, then backed off and turned to face the boy.

"Take it easy, son," he said. "I was checking to make sure she's all right."

"She is fine," Carl said. "I have come to bring her to our fire."

"Good idea," Parker said.

He walked away, and Carl appeared at her tent flap.

"*Are* you all right?" he asked.

"Yes," she said, "yes, I am all right. Thank you, Carl."

"Come," he said, "Papa says you should come to our fire and wait for your father."

"Yes, all right," she said. He helped her out of the wagon.

"You will be safe with us," Carl said.

"I know that, Carl," she said. "Thank you."

"You must stay away from Captain Parker," Carl said. "He is not a good man."

"He is the captain," she said as they walked. "Everyone depends on him."

"That does not give him the right to . . . to bother you," Carl said. He was a strapping young man of twenty, and it was his size that had no doubt caused the captain to back down.

But she was still afraid he would hurt Carl somehow.

"I will stay away from him," she said.

"Yes," Carl said, "but will he stay away from you?"

"We will see."

"What if we could make sure your daughter is safe?" Bullet said.

"How?" Talbot asked.

"Well, we could bring her to town, have someone watch over her," Bullet said.

"We would have to leave the wagon train," Talbot said. "Leave the others."

"You could catch up, once it was all over," Clint said.

"Perhaps," Talbot said.

"Maybe you should go back to the train and discuss it

with the others," Clint suggested. "I'm sure they'd all like to help solve this murder."

"When were you planning to leave?" Bullet asked.

"I believe the captain said we would leave tomorrow morning," Talbot said.

"Is it the captain's decision?" Clint asked. "Solely?"

"He is the captain," Talbot said. "Usually he makes those decisions."

"What's this about protecting your daughter from him?" Bullet asked.

Talbot seemed reluctant to answer.

"Come on, Mr. Talbot," Clint said. "We can't help you if you don't talk to us."

"I believe the captain . . . likes my daughter."

"Likes her?" Bullet asked.

"Lusts after her," the man said.

"How old is she?" Clint asked.

"Seventeen."

"Parker looks like he's in his forties," Clint said.

"Much too old for your daughter," Bullet said. "What's her name?"

"Sarah."

"Has she complained about his attention?"

"Yes, she has."

"Well," Clint said, "maybe it would help if I had a talk with the captain. I could get him to leave her alone."

"You would do that?"

"Sure," Clint said. He looked at Bullet. "Why don't we all ride back to the camp and talk about it."

"Actually, I'm gonna stay around here," Bullet said. "I want to see if anyone in town can identify the dead man."

"That would be helpful," Clint said. "Come on, Talbot. Let's see what we can do about the captain, and about making you feel better about helping us."

Talbot nodded, and they left the sheriff's office.

TEN

As Clint and Talbot rode out to the camp, Clint tried to learn more about the man.

"What did you do in your country?"

"I was a hunter."

"What kind of hunter?" Clint asked. "I mean, we have different kinds of hunters in this country. Animal hunters, manhunters—"

"Manhunters?" Talbot asked.

"Bounty hunters," Clint said.

"No," he said, shaking his head, "no, I was not a bounty hunter. Not really."

"Then what?"

"It is difficult to explain," Talbot said. "I would have to . . . show you."

"Show me how?"

"We can talk about that another time," Talbot said as they approached the wagon train camp. "I will have to . . . show you something."

"All right," Clint said. "Let's finish with this first."

As they rode up to camp, Sarah saw her father and ran to him.

"Papa!"

As he dismounted, he took her into his arms.

"Are you all right?" she asked.

"I am fine," he said. "How are you?"

"I am good," she said. "Carl has been looking after me. He and his father made me sit by their fire."

Talbot knew he'd have to thank Gerhardt for that. The man knew that Captain Parker was lusting after Sarah, and that Talbot did not want to say anything to the others. He was afraid if Parker found out, he would leave them stranded. He would probably take the guide with him, since it was he who had recommended him.

"That is good," Talbot said, holding her at arm's length.

"Are you back?" she asked. "Are we ready to move on?"

"Not yet, my dear," he said. "They want me to help them."

"Help them? How?"

"They want me to track their . . . killer."

"But why?" she asked. "Why should you help?"

"Because," he said, lowering his voice, "I know what the killer is."

Her eyes widened.

"Oh, no!"

"Yes."

"Here?" she asked. "In this country?"

He nodded.

"Were we . . . followed?"

"That is possible," he said. "If we were, if we brought this killer here, you can see why I must help them."

"But what about . . . the others?" she asked. "Will we have to leave them?"

"For a time, perhaps."

"But how—"

"Mr. Adams is here to help."

"What can he do?"

"He is a famous man in this country," Talbot said. "He will talk to the captain—"

"Papa—"

"Don't worry," he said. "Don't worry. It will be all right."

"Welcome back, Talbot," Captain Parker said.

"Captain," Talbot said, putting his arm protectively around Sarah.

"And Adams," Parker said. "What brings you back?"

"Actually," Clint said, "we're asking Mr. Talbot for a little more help, and it might make it necessary for him to leave the train for a time."

"Leave?" Parker frowned. "Do you expect us to wait for him?"

"No," Clint said, "we figure he can catch up."

"Well," Parker said, "if his daughter stays with us, we'll be sure to keep her safe."

"I wanted to talk to you about that," Clint said, putting his arm around the captain's shoulders. "Let's take a walk."

As Clint and Parker walked away, Gerhardt came over to Talbot.

"What is happening?" he asked. "What about this murder?"

"I think I will have to help them hunt the killer down," Talbot said.

Gerhardt's eyes widened.

"Is it . . ."

"It looks like," Talbot said. He explained about the wounds on the body and the tracks in the ground and the blood.

"Is it possible?" Gerhardt asked.

"I will have to find out."

"Why you, Papa?" Sarah asked.

"Because it may be my fault the killer is in this country, Sarah," Talbot said.

"But . . . you don't have your kit. You left it at home . . . or did you?"

Talbot looked at Gerhardt, who looked away.

"Didn't you?"

"No," he said, "no, I did not. I have it with me."

"Papa!" she said, stepping away from him. "But you promised."

"Sarah—"

"You said you would not hunt again," she went on. "You promised."

"I am sorry," he said, with a shrug, "I am a hunter. It is what I do."

"Sarah," Gerhardt said, "it is your papa's responsibility."

"Is it?" she demanded. "Even after it was his hunting that caused my momma to be killed?"

She turned and stormed away.

"Frederick," Gerhardt said, "if you leave the train . . ."

"I can take her with me and leave her in town," Talbot said, "or I can let her go with you. I will catch up later, when it is over."

"If you leave her with us," Gerhardt said, "we will keep her safe or die."

Talbot knew that.

But he was also afraid of that.

ELEVEN

"I don't know what you mean," Parker said to Clint.

"I think you do," Clint said. "Sarah Talbot is a lovely young woman."

"Yes, she is."

"And I think you should keep away from her."

"I don't know—"

"If I hear you bothered her," Clint said, "you'll have to deal with me. Do you understand?"

The color drained from the captain's face and he took a step away from Clint.

"Do you?" Clint demanded.

"Yes," Parker said hurriedly, "y-yes, I—I understand."

"Good," Clint said, slapping the man on the back firmly. "And I wouldn't want to hear that you abandoned these people."

"I wouldn't do that!" Parker said. "I have a reputation."

"Good," Clint said. "I'm glad we understand each other. We do understand each other, don't we, Captain? Completely?"

"Y-Yes," Parker said. "Completely."

When Clint returned to camp with the captain, the man slunk away.

"I don't think your Sarah will have any problem with the captain anymore," Clint said to Talbot.

"We were just discussing what would be best," Gerhardt said.

"This is my friend Gerhardt," Talbot said. "He and his son, Carl, have sworn to keep Sarah safe."

"Good," Clint said, "because I think she'd be safer staying with the wagons. Especially with a killer in the area."

"Agreed," Talbot said.

"Shall we go, then?" Clint asked.

"Just give me a moment."

Clint nodded and stood with Gerhardt while Talbot went to his wagon.

Talbot climbed into the back of his wagon and immediately went to the cedar chest, removing the blanket. He unlocked it and removed the vampire kit from inside. Then he reached behind him for a canvas bag that had a flap and a long handle that would allow him to wear it over his shoulder. He donned it, then opened the flap and fit the vampire kit inside, closing the flap after it.

Prepared for what he had to do, he climbed out of his wagon and looked around. There was no sign of Sarah, so he started over to his friend Gerhardt's fire.

Clint saw Talbot walking toward him, wearing a canvas bag over his shoulder with the big flap on it. He had no idea what was inside, but if the man wanted him to know, he'd tell him eventually.

"Are you ready?" Clint asked.

"Yes, I am ready." Talbot turned to Gerhardt and shook his hand.

"We'll keep her safe," his friend said again. "I promise you."

"I know you will."

"Go with God."

"I hope so," Talbot said with feeling. "I sincerely hope so."

Gerhardt looked at Clint and said, "Good luck to you, Mr. Adams."

"Thanks," Clint said as Talbot mounted his horse. "I think I'm going to need it."

Talbot and Clint turned their horses and rode back to Effingham.

TWELVE

When they got back to town, Clint got Talbot his own room at the hotel. He assured the dubious desk clerk that the town would be paying for it.

They went up to his room so he could leave his gear. He put the canvas bag on the bed and looked around.

"I have never been in such a room," Talbot said.

To Clint the room was much like any other hotel he'd ever been in. Nothing special.

To Frederick Talbot, it was a palace.

"I feel guilty being here while Sarah sleeps in the back of our wagon."

"We still have time to go and get her," Clint said. "They don't leave 'til morning."

"No, no," Talbot said, "she is safer there with the Gerhardts."

"All right, then," Clint said. "Let's go and find the sheriff."

"Yes, all right."

Talbot picked up his bag and slipped it over his head.

"No gun?" Clint asked.

"I have a gun," Talbot assured him, "but I will also need a rifle."

"We'll get you one," Clint said.

He looked at the bag as they left the hotel. Whatever was in it bulged, but he still didn't ask.

"What's in the bag?" Sheriff Bullet asked.

As Clint and Talbot entered the office, that was the first thing Bullet said.

"Just some items I will be needing," Talbot said.

"He'll need a rifle, Ray," Clint said.

"Take one off the rack."

Talbot went to the rack and immediately took down a Winchester.

"Never have I had such a rifle," he said.

"Well, you don't have it now," Bullet said. "But you can borrow it."

"Of course," Talbot said. "I will give it back when we are finished."

"Good," Bullet said.

"If we are still alive."

"And what's that supposed to mean?" Bullet asked.

"We are obviously going after a killer who enjoys killing," Talbot said. "In my experience they are the most difficult to catch."

"Just the same," Bullet said, "I'd appreciate a little more confidence than that."

"I understand," Talbot said, but he didn't go on to offer any.

Bullet looked at Clint.

"Are things squared away at the wagon train camp?" he asked.

"Pretty much," Clint said. "They're ready to pull out in the morning. We've tried to make arrangements to keep Talbot's daughter safe. But I have a question."

"What is it?"

"Are you ready to let them pull out?"

"Sure. Why not?"

"Do you think that one of them could be the killer?"

"No!" Talbot said.

They both looked at the Romanian.

"Why not?" Clint asked.

"I would not have brought my daughter along with this group if there was a killer among them."

"You'd be able to tell?" Bullet asked.

"Yes."

"How?"

"It is what I do."

Bullet looked at Clint for understanding, didn't seem to get it.

"Were you a lawman in your country?" the sheriff asked.

"No."

"He was a hunter," Clint offered.

"And you feel that you know a killer by lookin' at him?" Bullet asked.

"Yes, I do."

"As a lawman I sure wish I had that ability," Bullet said. He turned to Clint. "To answer your question, no, I don't think any of those people are the killer. I don't feel somebody could have gotten away from camp to commit this murder without being missed."

"I agree," Clint said.

"Did you get him a hotel room?"

"Yes."

"Then I think we should be ready to leave in the mornin'," Bullet said. "We'll go out to the site and start from there."

"I would like to walk around town," Talbot said.

"Lookin' for the killer?" Bullet asked.

"Just . . . walking," Talbot said.

"Fine with me," Bullet said. "We'll meet in front of the hotel at seven a.m."

Talbot nodded and looked at Clint.

"I'll see you at the hotel later," Clint said. "We'll get something to eat together."

"As you wish."

Talbot nodded, and left, taking the Winchester with him.

"So what's in the bag?" Bullet asked.

"I don't know," Clint said. "He hasn't shown me."

"Aren't you curious?"

"I am, but I'm waiting for him to tell me on his own," Clint said. "What did you find out here in town while we were gone?"

"Nothin'," Bullet said. "Nobody knows the dead man. He's a complete stranger."

"That's odd," Clint said. "Not a townie. And not with the train."

"I know. You really want to eat with this guy? He's . . . kind of weird."

"Yes, but there's something about him . . . I'm hoping I can get him to trust me and open up."

"Well, good luck," Bullet said. "I'll be eating on my own."

"So then I'll see you in the morning," Clint said.

"Here," Bullet said. He opened a desk drawer, came out with a box of Winchester shells, and tossed it to Clint, who caught it one-handed. "Give that to your friend."

Clint waved with the box and left the office.

THIRTEEN

Clint went back to the hotel, left the box of shells in his room. He'd give them to Talbot later.

He went back outside and stopped just in front of the hotel. He imagined Talbot walking around town, looking into people's faces to see if they were killers or not. Could he really tell? Was he that good?

He started to walk, found himself in front of Rita's dress shop. He hadn't seen Talbot at all up to here, but then he wasn't really looking for him. He decided to go inside.

A bell tinkled as he entered. There were two women at the counter—an older woman and a girl who was undoubtedly her daughter. Rita St. John looked over their shoulders at Clint, and smiled.

"Thank you so much, Rita," the older woman said. "You've been very helpful."

"It was my pleasure, Mrs. Rhodes. Good-bye, Amanda. Enjoy the dress."

"I will, ma'am," the girl said. When they turned around, Clint could see the daughter was about sixteen, and very pretty. The mother was about forty, and had been pretty at one time.

"Good day, ladies," he said, opening the door for them. Then he turned to Rita, still standing by the door.

"How's business?" he asked.

"Better than yesterday," she said. He could see that her breathing had already increased.

"Really? Then I guess you don't want me to do this." He turned the sign in the door window from OPEN to CLOSED, then looked at her again.

"I don't know," she said. "What did you have in mind?"

"I thought maybe you'd show me your storeroom."

"You want to see my storeroom?"

"Not really," he said, "but we could go back there anyway."

"Well," she said, "then follow me this way . . ."

He crossed the floor and followed her through a doorway into a back room filled with bolts of cloth of every color. As soon as they crossed the threshold, he grabbed her by the shoulders, turned her around, and gave her a kiss. Her mouth opened beneath his and they kissed avidly.

Clint didn't want to waste any time. He suddenly wanted her very badly. He lifted her, sat her on top of a crate, reached beneath her dress, and removed her underwear. Then he removed his gun belt and set it within reach, followed by his pants, which hit the floor. And then he was inside her, and she was gasping and clutching at him. This time, he had no concern for her pleasure, only for his own. He was going after a killer, and when you did that, the outcome was always uncertain. You never knew what lay ahead of you, or what you had to do to bring the killer to justice.

So he slammed in and out of her, over and over again, until finally she screamed and he exploded into her . . .

She straightened her clothing while he pulled his pants back on and strapped on his gun.

"My God!" she said. "What got into you?"

"I have to leave."

"Today?"

"In the morning," he said. "I have to leave to hunt for a killer."

"The murderer Sheriff Bullet mentioned this morning?" she asked.

"Yes."

"It's all over town today that the murder was very . . . gruesome," she said, cringing.

"It was."

"So it will be dangerous," she said. "Why do you have to go?"

"The sheriff's a friend of mine," he explained, "and he has no deputies."

"But you'll come back."

"Of course."

"How can you be sure?"

"I always come back."

"But . . ."

"But what?"

"One day you might not."

"Not today, though," he assured her. "Come on, walk me out."

They left the storeroom and went back to the shop. She walked him to the front door, where he turned the sign from CLOSED to OPEN.

He opened the door.

"Can I come to your hotel tonight?"

"No, not tonight," he said. "We have to get ready. I have a feeling I have a lot to learn."

"Will you come to me when you return?" she asked.

"I will," he said, "but even when I come back, I won't stay. It will be time for me to move on."

"I understand," she said. "I just need . . . one more time."

He smiled, said, "We can do that," and left.

FOURTEEN

He returned to the hotel, found Frederick Talbot in his room.

"Find anything?" he asked when the man opened his door.

"No," Talbot said, "the killer is not in town."

"The killer," Clint said. "You don't say he or she, just the killer."

"Can we eat?" Talbot asked. "I am very hungry."

"Sure, we can eat," Clint said. "Come on."

He took Talbot to a nearby café. Again, to him it was a small place to eat, but to Talbot it was a place for a feast.

There were others dining who gave them odd looks as they entered. Two strangers and a murder in town. Maybe they were involved.

People didn't know how right they were.

As they sat, Talbot put his bag down on the floor between himself and the wall. The waiter came over and they both ordered steak dinners.

While they were eating, Clint asked, "Okay, what's in the bag?"

"Just some items I will need."

"You said you had a gun, but needed a rifle. What kind of gun?"

Talbot hesitated, then said, "After we finish eating, I will show you."

"Why all the secrecy, Talbot?" Clint asked. "Why can't you talk about what kind of hunter you were in your country?"

"It is difficult . . . it would not be understood in your country."

"So it's some kind of animal that exists only in your country?"

"Would that that were the case," Talbot said.

"See," Clint said, "it's that kind of vagueness that makes people curious. Makes me curious. If we're going to ride together, trust each other with our lives—and let's face it, that's what we're doing—we need to know something about each other."

Talbot thought that over for a moment, then said, "Very well. I will listen."

"You want me to talk first?"

"I thought you suggested that."

"I didn't," Clint said, "but all right, I'll go first. But when I'm done, it's going to be your turn to talk."

"Yes."

"You agree?"

Talbot hesitated, then said, "Yes."

"Okay, then . . ."

It didn't take long to fill Talbot in on his background.

"Then your reputation is as someone who kills," Talbot summed it up.

"Unfortunately, yes," Clint said.

"A gunman."

"Yes."

"And you can walk your streets with impunity?" Talbot asked.

"I don't know about that," Clint said. "I walk the streets at my own peril."

"And men try to kill you?"

"All the time."

"And you survive?"

"Yes. . . so far."

Their plates had been cleared away and they were currently both working on pie and coffee. Talbot apparently found the apple pie he'd ordered to be a very rare delicacy. He savored each bite.

"All right," Clint said, pushing his plate away, very little in the way of remnants left of his own peach pie. "It's your turn. Talk."

Talbot hesitated, ate the last bite of his pie, and pushed his plate away. Slowly—with great reluctance—he leaned over, opened the flap of his bag, reached in, and brought out a small box containing a pistol, and six silver bullets, which he placed in the center of the table.

Clint leaned forward to look without touching, for the moment.

"Are those silver bullets?"

"Yes."

"And what kind of gun is that?"

"It is German."

"May I?"

The man hesitated, then said, "Of course."

Clint picked the pistol up out of the box and examined it thoroughly.

"And are those actually silver bullets?" he asked again. "Real silver?"

"They are."

Clint picked one up, turned it over in his fingers, then replaced it, and the pistol.

"Why silver bullets?" he asked.

"Because," Talbot said, slowly, "that is what it will take to kill this killer. Nothing else will work."

"How do you know?"

"Because I have hunted this killer before," Talbot said. "Many times."

"This same killer?"

Talbot hesitated, then said, "Not exactly the same but the same type."

"And what type is that?" Clint asked. "Some kind of huge wolf?"

"It could be."

"Well," Clint said, "if it *could* be, then what else *could* it be?"

Talbot hesitated again, took the time to close the box and replace it in the bag. It took him a while, as he seemed to be opening something else, careful not to let it slip from the bag.

"Come on, Talbot," Clint said, "what else is in the damn bag?"

"Let us go back to the hotel," Talbot said, "and I will show you."

FIFTEEN

They went back to the hotel to Talbot's room. Once inside, he put the bag on the bed, opened the flap, and brought out a larger box than he had in the café. He placed the box on the bed and stepped back.

"Open it."

Clint opened the box, saw the other items in Frederick Talbot's vampire kit. He picked up a vial of liquid and asked, "What's this?"

"Holy water."

He put it back, picked up one of the wooden stakes inside the box, tested the tip with his thumb, then picked up a hammer. He held the stake in his hand—the proper way, Talbot noticed—and tapped it on the end with the hammer. Then he placed them very carefully back in the box.

"I think I know what this is," Clint said, "but why don't you tell me?"

"It is my vampire kit."

"So in your country you hunt . . ."

"Vampires."

"And you believe the murder to have been committed by a vampire?"

"Possibly."

"What else could it be?"

"Well . . ."

"Come on, Talbot," Clint said, "don't stop now. What else did you hunt in your country?"

Talbot hesitated, licked his lips, then said, "Werewolves."

"I've heard stories about vampires and werewolves," Clint said. "According to the tracks you saw, which do you believe it to be?"

"According to the tracks," Talbot said, "a werewolf."

"The large animal tracks, right?"

"Yes."

"And the bare footprint?" Clint asked. "The man's before he turned into the wolf?"

"Yes."

Talbot seemed stunned by Clint's apparent understanding of these creatures.

Clint nodded, looked down at the open vampire kit on the bed.

"What are you thinking?" Talbot asked.

"I'll tell you what I should be thinking," Clint said. "That you're crazy."

"But you do not?"

"I won't say that," Clint said. "But you've obviously hunted something in your country that had committed this same kind of atrocity. And I saw what was done to that body. I'm not sure we have anything in this country that would do that. Not any one creature anyway."

"What will you tell the sheriff about this?" Talbot asked.

Clint closed the box and said, "Nothing. The sheriff would not have the same open mind that I do. He'd think you were crazy, and he would not let you come with us."

"But you will let me come."

"Yes."

Talbot took the box off the bed and put it back in the bag.

"But when we leave tomorrow," Clint said, "I want you to have that gun in your belt, not in its box."

"All right."

"Can you hit what you aim at with either gun?" Clint asked.

"Yes."

"Maybe when we get on the trail, we'll have a look," Clint said.

"That is fine."

Clint turned for the door, then turned back.

"Don't talk to anyone else about this."

"I will not."

Clint believed him. He knew, however, that in this country, everyone would think the man was crazy.

Well, almost everyone.

SIXTEEN

Back in his own room, Clint thought about the conversation he'd had with Frederick Talbot. And about what he had seen.

A vampire kit. He'd heard of such a thing, but had never seen it. Now that he had, he thought he needed a drink, but decided against leaving his room.

He took off his boots, hung his gun belt on the bedpost, and reclined on the bed, fully dressed.

Vampires?

Werewolves?

Legends, right? But here was a man from a country where such things were thought to exist. And this man had actually hunted them. He knew Ray Bullet would never believe such a thing. They were going to have to be careful never to let the lawman see the kit, or hear them talking about it. If he did, he'd probably turn right around and come back to town, convinced that they were both out of their minds.

He'd seen the tracks himself, now that Talbot had shown them to him. A bare foot in the blood, and a large animal print which could have been a wolf—or a werewolf.

They were going to have to follow the blood trail.

*   *   *

In the morning Clint got out before Talbot, went to the stable, and saddled both their horses. As he walked them back to the hotel, he saw Sheriff Bullet waiting in front with his own horse.

"I talked to the cook in the hotel dining room," Bullet told Clint. "He's making breakfast for us, even though they're not really open yet."

"I'd expect nothing less for a posse," Clint said. "Thanks."

They tied off the horses and went into the lobby to wait for Talbot.

"That horse of his gonna keep up?" Bullet asked.

"He says she will," Clint said.

"What did you fellas talk about last night?" the lawman asked.

"He didn't know much about my background," Clint said. "I filled him in."

"And what about his background?"

"He still says he's a hunter," Clint said. "Not much more."

"Can we trust him?"

"I think so."

"How good is he with a gun?"

"I thought we'd find out once we got out on the trail," Clint said, "but he's already proven himself as far as reading sign."

"I suppose you're right."

"What do we have in the way of supplies?"

"Bare minimum," Bullet said. "Coffee and hard tack. Maybe a bottle of whiskey."

"Maybe?"

"Yeah, okay," Bullet said. "A bottle of whiskey—for medicinal purposes."

"Of course."

At that point Talbot appeared in the stairway and came down to the lobby.

"Good morning," he said.

"Mornin'," Bullet said.

Talbot looked at Clint, who knew what he was thinking. Had he told Bullet about the night before?

"Ready for breakfast?" Clint asked.

"I did not think we would stop for breakfast. Yes. I am ready."

"Good. The sheriff arranged for them to cook for us here."

"Thank you," Talbot said to Bullet.

The three men went into the empty dining room and had their choice of tables. Clint allowed the sheriff to make the choice.

They all had steak and eggs and coffee. The cook also brought out a basket of warm biscuits.

"You get everything squared away with your daughter?" Bullet asked.

"Yes," Talbot said, "she will be quite safe while we are gone."

"That's good."

They started to eat and Bullet said, "I assume you'll want to start right from the site."

"Yes," Talbot said, "we will start to follow the blood trail from there."

"The blood trail?" Bullet asked.

"The tracks I found were left in blood," Talbot explained to them.

"Yes, but the killer's feet won't stay wet with blood for long."

"It is just a phrase," Talbot said.

"Oh, I see," Bullet said. "Okay."

Talbot looked at Clint, who tried to give him a look that said, *Your secret is safe with me.* Ray Bullet's face was buried in his plate, so he didn't notice.

SEVENTEEN

The killer watched from hiding as the wagons started to pack up to roll out.

The members of the train had no idea that he'd been observing them since the day before. They went about their business calmly, readying their wagons for the push west.

The killer's eyes followed Sarah Talbot in particular, since she was the spawn of the killer's sworn enemy.

"Come on, Sarah," Carl said. "We're ready to go."

She was staring off at something in the distance.

"What are you looking at?" Carl asked.

"I just feel . . ."

"What?"

She turned and looked at the young man, her arms folded, holding herself as if she was cold.

"I just feel as if I'm being watched," she explained to him.

"By who?"

"I don't know."

"Captain Parker?" he asked. "If he bothers you again, I will—"

"No, no," she said, "not him."

"Then who?"

She shook her head.

"Oh, never mind," she said. "Come on, we'd better get started."

Exasperated, Carl replied, "That is what I have been saying . . ."

The killer continued to watch from hiding as the wagons actually started to ride out. He was close enough to smell them, especially the girl.

As the last wagon left the camp, he waited, watching until they were in the distance. Only then did he leave his hiding place and move into the deserted camp.

He still had not decided whether to follow them—follow his hated enemy's female child—or go after the enemy instead. He moved only after careful consideration.

Or perhaps, he would simply allow the enemy and his companions to chase him . . . until they were the ones who were caught.

EIGHTEEN

Clint, Talbot, and the sheriff mounted their horses and rode out of town. Talbot took the lead and led them back to the site of the murder.

Once again Talbot dismounted and walked the ground.

"Didn't he do this already?" Bullet asked.

"He just wants to make sure," Clint said.

Talbot rejoined them and mounted up.

"It's this way," he said.

"What are we followin'?" Bullet asked. "The human tracks or the animal tracks?"

"Both," Talbot said, and rode ahead.

"What?" Bullet said to Clint, who just shrugged.

"We better follow him."

Along the way, Bullet asked, "So what's in the bag?"

"I still don't know."

"Didn't you ask him?"

"No."

"Why not?"

"I haven't asked you what's in your saddlebags, have I?"

"Well, no, but . . ."

"If he wants us to know," Clint said, "if it's important, he'll tell us sometime."

"I can't help but wonder," Bullet said. "It's a weird-lookin' bag."

Clint didn't comment.

"In fact, that guy is weird."

"How so?"

"Foreign," Bullet said. "They're all foreign. Germans, Polish—what do they call them, Poles? Poles. And this fella, he's from . . . where?"

"Romania."

"Where is that?"

"I don't know," Clint said. "I haven't looked at a map."

"And what do they have there that he used to hunt?" Bullet asked. "What kind of animals?"

"I haven't asked him that either."

"Ain't you friends with him?"

"No," Clint said, "I'm friends with you, Ray. I just met Talbot, like you did."

"Yeah, but you make friends fast."

They camped at dusk, and Clint decided to have Talbot shoot before it got dark. The man claimed to be able to hit what he aimed at, but Clint would feel better if he could see it for himself.

"Just for my peace of mind," he explained, "I need to see that you really can hit what you aim at."

"What would you like me to shoot?" Talbot asked while Bullet built a fire.

Clint looked around, then picked out a likely target, something pretty simple.

"That cottonwood tree."

"Which branch?"

"Just hit the tree," Clint said. "I don't want you to be a sharpshooter, I just want you to be able to hit it."

Talbot raised the rifle and fired, stuck the trunk of the tree dead center.

Clint leaned over to look past Talbot at Bullet and asked, "Good enough?"

"Have him do it one more time," Bullet said, putting on a pot of coffee. "Just in case it was a fluke."

Talbot fired the rifle again with the same results.

"Good enough?" Clint asked the lawman.

"Good enough," Sheriff Bullet said. "Come and have your hardtack dinner."

NINETEEN

They sat around the fire, washing down beef jerky with coffee.

"The coffee is very good," Talbot said.

"It's the way he likes it," Bullet said. "Strong enough to clean your gun with."

"Don't let him fool you," Clint said. "He likes my trail coffee, too."

"I would like some more," Talbot admitted.

Clint filled his tin cup.

"How does the trail look, Talbot?" Bullet asked.

"It is faint."

"But you can see it?"

"Of course."

Bullet looked at Clint.

"We'll have to take his word for it," Clint said. "I can't see it myself."

"It is there," Talbot assured them. "Do not worry."

"Worryin' is my job," Bullet said.

"Well, then . . ." Talbot said.

"Well, then . . . what?"

"We have been circling."

"What? Goin' in circles?"

"Not in circles," Talbot said. "Circling."

"What's it mean, Talbot?" Clint asked.

"The killer is not sure where to go," Talbot said.

"When will he figure it out?" Bullet asked.

"I expect his trail to take a definite direction tomorrow."

"If he circles back to town . . ." Bullet said.

"He will not."

"What makes you think so?" Bullet asked.

"There is no one in town it wants to kill."

"The killer wants to kill somebody?" Bullet asked. "You don't think the murder was random?"

"No."

"Then why did he kill that man?"

"I am not sure, but . . ."

"But . . ." Bullet looked at Clint. "How much do you think this man is holdin' out on us?"

"I am not . . . holding out," Talbot said. "I am just thinking."

"And what has your thinking come up with?"

"The clothes the dead man was wearing."

"Yes?"

"They were European."

"How can you be sure?"

"Because they were like what I wear," Talbot said. "My clothes are sewn, and sewn again when they need it. I never have new clothes. Neither did the dead man."

"So he's from your country?"

"That I don't know," Talbot said. "He could have been German, or Russian—"

"Russian? Why bring them into it?" Bullet asked.

"Very well," Talbot said. "German, or Polish, or . . . Romanian."

"What are Romanians called?" Clint asked.

"Roma," Talbot said, "or Romanies. The Romanies are Gypsies. That is what I am."

"Gypsies," Bullet repeated. "Aren't they thieves?"

"Ray!" Clint said.

"It is all right," Talbot said. "Some Gypsies are thieves, just as some Americans are."

"You're sayin' Americans and Gypsies are the same?" Bullet asked.

"I am saying we are all the same," Talbot said. "Most of us."

They set a three-man watch, although Bullet still didn't trust Talbot completely.

"I'll sleep with one eye open during his watch," he told Clint.

"That'll make two of us."

Bullet turned and looked over his shoulder at Talbot, who was already sprawled out, asleep on the ground.

"You don't trust him either?"

"Let's just say I'm careful," Clint said.

"You and me, we gotta watch each other's back," the lawman said.

"Agreed."

"You think he's tellin' the truth? About the killer circlin'?"

"Why would he lie?"

"I don't know." He slapped Clint on the back. "I'm just bein' careful. Wake me in three."

"See you later, Ray," Clint said.

Sheriff Bullet waved and rolled himself up in his own bedroll.

Clint poured himself another cup of coffee, looked over at Talbot, who seemed to be sleeping comfortably.

Frederick Talbot slept with one eye open. He always did.

TWENTY

In the morning they got on the trail again.

"Widening," Talbot said as they went. "An ever-widening circle."

"Why would he do that?" Bullet asked.

"Some creatures circle their prey before striking," Talbot said.

He rode on ahead. Bullet looked at Clint.

"Creatures," Bullet said. "Why would he use that word?"

"That's just the way he talks."

"We still don't know if we're trailin' a man or an animal."

"Maybe both," Clint said.

"Both," Bullet said. "So you mean, it might be a man with a wolf he can control?"

"Or a wolf he can't control," Clint said.

"Then why wouldn't it kill him?" Bullet asked.

"I don't know," Clint said. "I'm just thinking out loud."

Clint and Bullet rode up on Talbot as the man reined in and stood in his stirrups.

"What is it?" Clint asked.

"Oh, no," the Romanian said.

"What?" Bullet asked.

"There," Talbot said, "it's there."

He kicked his horse in the withers and took off running. Clint and Bullet pursued him. Finally the man came to a stop in what looked like a cold camp.

"I know this place," Clint said, looking around. There were several cold fires, a lot of footprints . . . and wagon tracks.

"Oh, yeah," Bullet said. "This is where all the wagons were camped."

Talbot had dismounted and was walking around, frantically studying the ground.

"What the hell—" Bullet started.

"Give him some time," Clint said.

Talbot continued to walk about, looking aimless and panicked. Finally, he turned to Clint and Bullet, walked up to them.

"It's following them."

"Following who?" Bullet asked.

"The wagons," Talbot said. "My friends. My daughter. It's following them."

"It?" Bullet asked. "Man or beast?"

Talbot licked his lips, said, "Maybe both."

"Now that's what Clint said to me," Bullet said. "Maybe both. What's that mean?"

"It means we must get moving," Talbot said. "They have a head start of a day."

"They're movin' slow," Bullet said. "We got time to catch up."

"But don't you see?" Talbot asked. "If we have time to catch them, it also has a head start."

"Now, Mr. Talbot," Bullet said, dismounting, "I ain't ridin' another foot until you tell me what 'it' is. Or what you think 'it' is."

"Mr. Adams—" Talbot said. "We must hurry!"

"Tell him, Talbot," Clint said. "He has a right to know."

"Tell me," Bullet said. "You already know?"

"I know," Clint said.

"And you didn't tell me? Why?"

"You'll see," Clint said. He looked at Talbot. "Tell him."

TWENTY-ONE

"That's crazy!" Bullet said.

He was looking at Talbot's vampire kit, which was open on the ground. Then he looked at Clint. "That's crazy."

"Maybe it is," Clint said. "But that doesn't mean he can't track what we're after."

"What? Or who?" Bullet asked. "Which is it?"

Clint shrugged.

"I guess we'll find that out when we catch it."

"You're still willin' to follow this fella who thinks he hunts vampires?"

"Whether we're hunting a vampire or not, Ray," Clint said, "we're hunting something, something that tore a man apart. So we need all the help we can get."

Bullet stared at Talbot, who looked extremely worried.

"There are no tracks of a horse, right?" Bullet asked.

"No," Talbot said.

"Then how is this killer going to catch up to them?" the lawman asked.

Talbot didn't answer.

Bullet looked at Clint.

"Don't tell me," he said.

Clint shrugged. "I guess he'll run."

"And what can run that fast," Bullet asked, "a vampire or a werewolf?"

"Either one, I guess," Clint said.

"Ahhh," Bullet said in disgust.

Talbot and Clint waited, then Clint asked, "What are we going to do, Ray?"

Bullet, still looking disgusted, said, "Mount up!"

Talbot hurriedly climbed atop his horse before the lawman could change his mind.

They rode for half a day, pushing, but they were only as fast as their slowest horse and—remarkably—that proved to be the sheriff's horse, not Talbot's old mare.

"We're not gonna catch up to them today," Bullet said.

"Mr. Adams can," Talbot said. "With his horse, he could ride until he catches them."

"I don't know this country," Clint said, "and I'm not putting Eclipse at risk by riding him at night."

"That's it," Bullet said. "We'll camp and get an early start."

"But my daughter—"

"Your daughter is safe with the people in the train," Bullet said. "You said that yourself."

"Yes, but not against . . ."

"Against what?"

"This," Talbot said. "Not against this."

"Will it charge into the camp after all those people?" Bullet asked.

"There's no telling—"

"What does it usually do?"

"Normally," Talbot said, "it will prey on the weak when they are alone."

"And is your daughter likely to be alone?"

"No."

"That's it, then," Bullet said. "No more discussion."

They set up camp, Bullet building the fire, Clint picketing the horses. Talbot just sat on a rock, looking worried.

Bullet put on the coffee and handed out the hardtack. Talbot nibbled with no interest.

"Don't worry, Talbot," Clint said. "We'll catch them tomorrow."

"It may be too late," Talbot said. He shook his head. "I never should have left her."

Clint could see how worried the man was and sought to put his mind at ease.

"You had no way of knowing this killer would go after the wagons—"

"I should have realized it!" Talbot said bitterly.

"Why?" Clint asked. "How?"

"Because this killer must be from my country!"

"If that's the case, how did it get here?"

"The same way I did."

"You mean . . . the same way, or the same boat?" Clint asked.

"Either one," Talbot said.

Clint leaned forward. Bullet was remaining silent, just listening.

"Are you thinking this thing followed you here?" Clint asked. "That it's here . . . for you?"

"It is very possible."

"This is crazy," Bullet said into his coffee.

"Crazy or not," Clint said, "we're on the trail of a killer. That's all that matters."

"Saving my daughter is all that matters!" Talbot said forcefully.

Clint found that he couldn't honestly disagree with him.

TWENTY-TWO

The killer sniffed the air, could smell the girl. But she was in camp, with all the others, sitting next to a fire.

The killer sat and quietly, patiently waited for one of them to separate from the others. If he could just get one of them alone . . .

Sarah still had the uncomfortable feeling they were being watched. The feeling manifested itself as a chill that ran up her spine and down her arms. It made her feel so cold.

She jumped as something touched her shoulders, then realized it was Carl, putting a blanket around her.

"You are cold," he said. "This should help."

"Thank you."

"And get closer to the fire."

She knew it wouldn't help any more than the blanket did, but for his benefit she scooted a little closer.

"Better?" he asked hopefully.

"Better," she lied.

He sat across the fire from her.

"Are you worried about your father?"

"Yes."

"Do not worry, Sarah," Carl said. "Your father is a great hunter."

"He was a great hunter," she said. "When my mother was killed, he lost his taste for it, and we came to this country, where he thought he would not have to hunt ever again. And now . . ." "Perhaps this killer is not what your father thinks it is," Carl offered.

"I am afraid my father knows," she said.

"He knows what the killer is?"

"I do not mean he actually knows what it is," she replied, "but he knows what they are hunting for. He is always able to tell."

"Then he will catch it," Carl said, "and he will kill it. And then he will come back to you."

"I hope you are right, Carl," Sarah said.

Carl's father came over and said, "Carl, we need water. There is a stream nearby."

"Yes, sir." The young man looked at Sarah. "I will be right back."

But he wasn't.

TWENTY-THREE

In the morning they rose, had some coffee, and then broke camp. Talbot was eager—no, frantic—to get going, and hurriedly killed the fire by pouring the remainder of the coffee on it.

They saddled their horses and mounted up.

"We have all day," Bullet told them. "No need to push the horses too hard."

"But we must catch up to them!"

"We will," Clint said, "but not by killing the horses."

Talbot took a deep breath. "Yes, all right."

They started out. Talbot still took the lead, even though they could all see the tracks left by the wagons.

"He's about to jump out of his skin," Bullet said. "He does and the great vampire hunter won't be doing us any good."

"He'll be okay," Clint said.

"What makes you so sure?"

"He's lived this long," Clint said, "and he wants to save his daughter."

"We all want to save his daughter," Bullet said. "I don't want to see anyone else die, but . . ."

"But what?"

"I can't deal with this, Clint," Bullet said. "When we

catch up to them, are they all also gonna believe in vampires and werewolves?"

"I don't know," Clint said. "Why don't we wait until we catch up to see?"

They rode at a pace set by Talbot and his mare. The wheel tracks were getting fresher and Talbot was getting more anxious.

"No graves along the way," Clint said.

"What?" Talbot asked.

"If anything had happened already," Clint said, "we would have seen gravesites along the way."

"I suppose you are correct," Talbot said.

"That was supposed to make him feel better?" Bullet asked.

"It was worth a try," Clint said.

"The only thing that's gonna make him feel better is to see his daughter, alive," the lawman said.

"Let's hope," Clint said.

An hour later they came to a cold campsite, and a grave.

"Oh, no," Talbot said.

Clint dismounted and walked to it. It was marked by a cross made from two sticks. There was no way to tell if a man or woman was buried there.

"Pretty fresh," he said. "They must've camped last night, and this happened."

"Maybe," Bullet said, "somebody just died. You know, natural causes."

Talbot looked as if he was about to panic.

"Take it easy, Talbot," Clint said. "Don't fall apart until we know."

"Yes," Talbot said, "you are right."

It was almost dusk when Bullet said, "We're gonna have to stop."

"They have to stop, too," Clint said. "I think we can find their camp."

"You're the one who doesn't want to risk your horse in the dark," Bullet reminded him.

"I know," Clint said, "but we've still got some time. Let's push on a bit."

"Yeah, okay," Bullet said.

"Thank you," Talbot said to Clint.

"But just a little while," Bullet said.

"I understand."

Fifteen minutes later Talbot asked, "Smell that?"

They sniffed the air.

"No," Bullet said.

"Yes," Clint said. "A campfire."

"Fires," Talbot said. "More than one. Just up ahead."

"Then let's go," Clint said.

The killer had just about decided to go ahead and move into camp when the riders came along. He sniffed, smelled danger, but also smelled something—*someone*—familiar.

He backed into the brush and settled down to wait patiently.

TWENTY-FOUR

When Talbot saw the wagons and the fires, he urged his horse into a gallop.

"Sarah!" he screamed. "Sarah!"

"Papa?"

The girl came running toward him. He dismounted and ran to grab her and hold her tightly.

"Looks like the girl's okay," Bullet said.

"Yeah," Clint said.

Gerhardt approached the two mounted men.

"Mr. Gerhardt," Clint said. "We saw the grave. Who died?"

"My son," the man said sadly.

"I'm sorry," Clint said.

"How did he die?" Bullet asked.

"The same way the other man did," Gerhardt said. "He was torn apart."

"Jesus," Bullet said.

Clint dismounted, followed by the lawman.

"We tracked it," Clint said. "I mean, Talbot tracked it, found out it was following the wagon train . . . whatever it is."

"Varcolac!" Gerhardt cried out suddenly, looking close to tears.

"What?" Clint asked.

"What does that mean?" Bullet asked.

"Several things," Gerhardt said hoarsely, trying to compose himself. "It could mean goblin . . . or vampire . . . or werewolf."

"Werewolf," Bullet said.

"Which do you think it was, Mr. Gerhardt?"

"From the condition of my son's body . . . what was left of it . . . *werewolf.*"

"Does everybody here believe that?" Bullet asked him.

"No," Gerhardt admitted. "Talbot and I are from Romania. We believe. Others—Germans, Poles—do not. Not all of them."

"Well, that's a relief," Bullet said to Clint. "At least some of these people are being realistic."

"Come," Gerhardt said, "we have food ready. There is plenty."

"We'll have to take care of our horses first," Clint said. "Thank you."

Gerhardt nodded, turned, and went back to the fire, where Talbot and his daughter were still hugging each other.

Clint and Bullet walked their horses and Talbot's to the picket line and unsaddled them.

"Maybe some of these people will have some other idea," Bullet said.

"Whatever their ideas are," Clint said, "let's not call them crazy, okay, Ray?"

"Huh? Oh, yeah, sure," Bullet said, then added, "even though some of them might be."

TWENTY-FIVE

They sat around the fire with Gerhardt and some of the others—Talbot and Sarah still sitting close together. Clint and Bullet listened while Gerhardt told them what happened.

"I sent the boy to get some water," he said. "When he didn't come back, we went looking for him. It was dark, we used torches. It took most of the night but we found him—what was left of him."

"So much blood," another man, Klaus Mueller, said, shaking his head sadly.

Sheriff Bullet asked him, "What do you think killed the boy?"

"I do not know," Mueller said in heavily accented English, "an animal of some sort."

"An animal," Bullet said. "A wolf?"

"Maybe."

"Not a werewolf?"

"Werwolf?" the man said in German. "I have never seen such a thing."

"But do you believe in them?"

"In the old country, perhaps," the man said, "but not here."

"We buried him," Gerhardt said. "The . . . pieces."

"We're so sorry," Clint said.

Talbot reached out and put his hand on his friend's shoulder. At that moment Captain Parker came over to join their circle.

"Sheriff," he said, "you've got to do somethin'."

"Like what?"

"Catch this maniac," Parker said. "He's after my train."

"Maybe," Bullet said. "In the morning' we'll have a look around."

"You gotta catch him," Parker said, "or it. It's your job to protect us."

"I thought it was your job to protect these people," Clint said.

"Huh? It's my job to get them where they're goin'," Parker said. "I didn't get paid to hunt some kinda wolf. I ain't a hunter."

"I am, Captain," Talbot said. "Do not worry. I will find it."

"Yeah, don't worry, Captain," Bullet said. "We'll find it."

"Well . . . can we pull out in the mornin'?" the captain asked.

"Sure, why not," Bullet asked. "We'll ride with you for a while."

"Fine," Parker said, "that's fine."

He walked away, back to the front of the train, where he sat at his own fire.

"The man is a coward," Gerhardt said. "He will leave us soon. Run away. If this thing is not stopped."

"Do not worry, my friend," Talbot said. "I will stop it."

"I will go with you," Gerhardt said.

"I have the sheriff and Mr. Adams," Talbot said. "You should stay with the train. We cannot trust Captain Parker to protect our people."

"You expect me to protect them?" Gerhardt asked. "I could not even protect my own son."

"You protected my daughter," Talbot reminded him.

Gerhardt looked at Sarah, then said to Talbot, "I love her like she was my own. I will protect her."

"Good," Talbot said. He looked at Clint and Bullet. "We will start in the morning."

After everyone on the train had turned in, Clint and Talbot remained awake, on watch. They had decided to watch two-by-two. In a while they would wake Bullet and Gerhardt.

Clint picked the coffeepot up from the fire and poured two cups. The other fires were starting to wink out.

"Perhaps," Talbot said, "we could get the sheriff to stay with the train tomorrow while we go hunting."

"Why?"

"He doesn't believe."

"I don't either."

"You have an open mind, Mr. Adams."

"Call me Clint."

"You have an open mind, Clint," Talbot said. "The sheriff is closed."

"That may be, but he thinks it's his job to find the killer."

"It is my destiny," Talbot said. "That comes before his job."

"And me?" Clint asked.

"You know what your destiny is," Talbot said. "But you will help me, because that is the kind of man you are."

"Are you sure?"

"I am very sure."

"Well," Clint said, sipping his coffee, "I guess we'll see."

The killer watched as the wagon train began to bed down—except for two of them.

The first was his foe, the hunter. The other man was even more of a danger.

More watching . . .

* * *

Talbot walked to the other end of the train, leaving Clint by
the fire. He drank coffee and looked out into the darkness.
Was there something there? Not that he could see anything,
but he had a feeling . . . and he always put great stock in his
feelings. They had kept him alive this long.

"I have that feeling, too, I'm afraid," Sarah said from
behind him.

Clint turned and saw her standing there.

"Your father will be back any minute," he said.

"You feel it, too, don't you?" she asked. "It's watching us."

"Do you think so?"

"I know so." She hugged her upper arms.

Clint walked up to her.

"You'd better go to bed," he said. "You need your rest."

"Don't let it kill my father," she whispered. "Don't let it."

"I won't," he promised, wondering if that was a promise
he'd be able to keep.

———

TWENTY-SIX

Clint woke up in the morning before most of the train's people. He rolled out from where he'd been sleeping beneath a wagon and stood up. It was Talbot's wagon, the one he had walked Sarah to the night before. Talbot had also been asleep underneath it, but he was gone already.

Soon other people began to rise. Women went to the fires to prepare the morning meal.

As Clint walked to one of the fires, Gerhardt turned to him and said, "He's gone. Left during the night."

"Who? Talbot?"

"No," Gerhardt said, "Captain Parker. He left, took his horse and some supplies. The coward has run."

"And the guide?"

"Him, too," Gerhardt said. "We are on our own."

"Don't worry," Clint said. "You'll get where you're going. Where is Talbot? And the sheriff?"

"They are around somewhere," Gerhardt said.

"And Sarah?"

"She has not come out of her wagon yet."

But at that moment she did, and came running to the fire.

"I am sorry," she said. "I overslept. I will start the morning meal."

"Don't worry about it," Clint said.

"Where's my father?" she asked.

Clint was about to say he didn't know when Talbot came walking up to the fire.

"Here he is."

"Good morning, Papa."

"Good morning, Sarah. Where is breakfast?"

"I am about to start it," she said. "Are you hungry?"

"Starving."

She smiled and set about preparing the meal.

Talbot took Clint's elbow and walked him a few feet away.

"What is it?"

"I had the feeling last night that we were being watched," Talbot said.

"So did I," Clint said. "Sarah felt the same way."

"Yes," Talbot said, nodding, "she has what you and I have."

"And what's that?" Clint asked.

"The instinct."

"And what does the instinct tell you?"

"Just so much," Talbot said. "For the rest I had to go and have a look."

"And?"

"I found tracks out there in the brush," he said. "He was watching us, possibly all night."

"And now?"

"No," Talbot said, "not now, not in the daylight."

"What do you suggest?" Clint asked.

"The same thing I suggested last night," Talbot said. "That the sheriff accompany the wagons while you and I hunt."

"Well, you'll have to make that suggestion to the sheriff," Clint said. "I think he'll have something to say about that."

"I shall do so, at breakfast," Talbot said.

They turned and walked back to the fire.

* * *

"I can't do that," Sheriff Bullet said.

"Why not?" Talbot asked.

They were seated around the fire, eating the bacon and beans Sarah had prepared for their morning meal.

"Well, for one thing," Bullet said, "I'm the sheriff of my county. Technically, I can't leave it. Not and have any authority. I need to catch the killer before it gets too far away."

"But you're already out of the county," Clint pointed out.

"I know the sheriff of this county," Bullet said. "We've worked together before. He'll vouch for me. But I'm not going to be able to go further."

"So what do you suggest?" Clint asked.

"Let Talbot here go with the wagon, and his people," Bullet said. "You and I can go hunting."

"But Talbot's the hunter," Clint pointed out, "and the tracker."

Bullet considered that for a moment.

"Well . . . you could go with the wagons, while I hunt with Talbot."

"I would prefer to hunt with Mr. Adams," Talbot said quietly but firmly.

"Why?" Bullet asked.

"He and I are the same."

"Is that a fact?"

"We have the same instincts," Talbot said. "We would keep each other alive."

"And I couldn't do that?"

Talbot didn't answer.

"Okay, but damn it," Bullet said, "there's got to be another way."

"There is," Clint said.

"What's that?"

"You go back to Effingham and resume your job," Clint told him.

"And you?"

"Talbot and I will travel with the wagons," Clint said. "If it's true that the killer is following this train, you won't have any further trouble."

"But you will."

"When Talbot and I have taken care of the situation, I'll telegraph you and let you know that your murder has been solved."

"That doesn't—that doesn't sound right."

"But it's the only way," Clint said.

Sheriff Bullet chewed his food and considered Clint's words.

"It makes sense," Talbot said.

"I know, damn it!" Bullet said. He looked at Clint. "I got you messed up in this. It doesn't feel right leaving you to handle it."

"Don't worry, Ray," Clint said. "If I wanted out, I'd ride out. Believe me."

"Yes," Bullet said, "yes, all right. It does seem the only solution. I'll head back to town after breakfast. But you have to keep me informed and let me know when you catch the killer."

"I will," Clint promised.

"And," Bullet said, "you have to tell me what the hell it is!"

TWENTY-SEVEN

Bullet rode out and headed back to Effingham.

Clint turned to Talbot, Gerhardt, Mueller, and the other members of the wagon train.

"So," he asked, "where are we headed?"

"Nevada," Gerhardt said. "We bought some property there. There is enough for all of us to settle on."

"You have paperwork?" Clint asked. He'd known of a lot of Easterners who had bought property in the West, only to find out upon their arrival that they'd been swindled. Either the seller never owned the property, or it was barren land that could not be worked.

"We do," Gerhardt said.

"Maybe you'll let me have a look?"

"Of course. I'll get it."

Gerhardt went to his wagon.

"Can we really make it?" Mueller asked. "Without Captain Parker, and the guide, and . . . a killer following us?"

"We will make it," Talbot said.

"I'll see to it," Clint said. "I was ready to leave Effingham and head west anyway. I'll get you all where you're going."

Talbot turned to the people and said, "Get your wagons ready to go."

The people—thirty men, women, and children—dispersed to get themselves ready to travel.

Talbot turned to Clint.

"I am very grateful," he said. "I would not hold it against you if you rode off with the sheriff."

"It's true that Bullet got me involved," Clint said, "but I'm in it now for the long haul. I don't want to see anyone else get killed."

"And you are curious, eh?" Talbot asked. "About who or what this killer is?"

"I have to admit," Clint said, "I do want to see who the killer is."

"You will," Talbot said.

Gerhardt came walking up, carrying some papers.

"Here they are."

Clint perused the papers. They looked like legitimate deeds, but of course it all depended on whether or not the seller had been legitimate. At the bottom of each page were half a dozen signatures.

"These wagons represent ten families who left Pennsylvania together," Gerhardt explained, accepting the papers back.

"They look okay," Clint said, "but I guess we'll find out for sure when we get there. You better get your wagon ready to travel, Mr. Gerhardt."

"Yes."

The man hurried back to his wagon. Clint walked over to Eclipse and saddled him, then saddled Talbot's horse for him.

Talbot came over and said, "I will ride in the wagon with Sarah for a while."

"Okay," Clint said, "I'll tie your saddle mount to the back of your wagon."

Clint saw Talbot's gun tucked into his belt.

"I'm glad to see you're carrying your pistol," Clint said. "Fully loaded with silver bullets?"

"Yes," Talbot said, touching the gun. "I want to be ready. I have a mold to make other bullets. I can make some for your gun, if you like."

"That's okay," Clint said. "I'm not buying into the whole silver bullet thing . . . not yet."

"I wish you would," Talbot said, "but I understand."

"Thanks for that."

"No, thank you," Talbot said.

"For what?"

"For not thinking I am a crazy man," the Romanian said. "For not telling the sheriff that I am crazy. For not walking away when you had the chance."

"Listen," Clint said, "you might just be crazy, Talbot, but I still think you're the best bet to catch this . . . killer."

"In that case," Talbot said, "I think perhaps you should start to call me Frederick."

"Okay," Clint said, "and you call me Clint."

The two men shook hands, as if meeting for the first time.

"I better take the lead," Clint said. "You go and get aboard your wagon."

"Yes."

"Who is in the lead wagon?"

"Gerhardt."

"Okay," Clint said. "Let's get rolling."

TWENTY-EIGHT

The wagon train started west again with Clint Adams in the lead. He had now gone from unofficial deputy to unofficial wagon master. Once again he'd stepped into other people's business and come away with the burden of seeing that things went right. He now had to not only find and stop a killer, but see that these people got to Nevada, where they may or may not have had a legitimate claim to some land.

They had all put their lives in his hands—or into the hands of him and Frederick Talbot.

And maybe he'd put his life into the hands of a crazy man. That remained to be seen, as well.

Frederick Talbot held the reins of his team loosely in his hands. His daughter, Sarah, sat next to him, holding tightly to his arm. She was so glad he was back, and he knew it. He was trying to put her mind at rest for the time being before he and Clint went out again, hunting. He knew that would upset her once more, but he was the only one who had a chance to catch and kill the monster, and he had a better chance with Clint's help. He just wished Clint had allowed him to make some silver bullets for his gun.

"Papa?"

"Yes, Sarah?"

"What are you thinking about?"

"Just the new life we're going to have in Nevada, Sarah," he lied. "That's all."

The killer watched as the wagon train pulled out. There was a new leader, and he was the dangerous one. The killer sensed that. There were only two in this group who were hunters. The rest were just prey.

His prey.

They traveled the day without incident, and then Clint called them to a halt.

"We'll camp here," he told Gerhardt, and then rode back to tell the others.

Once they had stopped and secured their stock and their wagons, Clint gathered them together.

"I only want two fires, and I want them close together," Clint said. "No one is to leave camp alone. Only in twos. And keep your children close."

"I hear a stream nearby," one of the women said. "We need water."

"Two of the men will go and get it," Clint said. "Make sure you're both armed."

Everyone agreed. They built two fires and the women started to prepare the meal.

"Who's going for water?" Clint called out.

"I am," Mueller said.

"I'll go with you."

That seemed to please Mueller. He picked up two buckets and they started to walk.

"I've got to ask you something," Clint said.

"What is that?"

"Do you believe in vampires and werewolves?"

"Of course not . . ."

"Well—"

"But I am from Germany," Mueller went on. "Those in our group who are from Romania, they believe wholeheartedly. Especially Talbot."

"Why Talbot?"

"Because he has hunted them," Mueller said.

"And you believe that?"

Mueller shrugged. "He says he has not only hunted them, but caught and killed them. Gerhardt supports his stories."

"But you have never seen one."

"No," Mueller said, "but that does not mean they do not exist."

They reached the stream and Mueller filled the two buckets of water. Clint took one from him and they walked back to camp. He carried the bucket in his left hand, leaving his gun hand free.

When they reached the camp, Clint went to one of the fires and accepted a cup of coffee from Sarah Talbot.

"Do you believe my father?"

"Sarah—"

"I can understand that you have never seen a vampire or a werewolf," she said, "but he has. He does not lie."

"I don't think he's lying," Clint said.

"Then you do believe him."

"I'm willing to follow him, and back him," Clint said. "I'm not ready yet to decide to believe in those creatures."

"Well," she said, "I am very grateful that you are here, and that Captain Parker is not." She reached out, put her hand on his, and looked into his eyes. "We need you."

For a moment, as he stared back at her, he did not see the eyes of a child, but of a woman. In fact, the look she gave him was feverish.

He started to wonder about Captain Parker, and if he might not have been pulled in by those eyes?

"Thank you for the coffee, Sarah," he said.

"Come back," she said. "The food will be ready very soon."

Clint walked away and encountered Frederick Talbot, who also had a cup of coffee.

"She is very frightened," Talbot said. "And is being very brave."

"Yes," Clint said, for want of anything else to say. The girl he'd just spoken to did not seem to be very frightened. He was starting to wonder how well Talbot knew his own daughter.

He looked at Talbot, who had suddenly stood stock-still. Only his eyes were moving.

"Do you feel it?" he asked.

"What?"

"We are being hunted."

"I'd much rather be the hunter," Clint said.

"So would I. Perhaps that is what we should do," Talbot said.

"What are you suggesting?" Clint asked.

"After everyone else has retired for the night," Talbot said, "perhaps you and I should go out and do what we do best—hunt."

"In the dark?" Clint asked. "Wouldn't that be playing right into the hands of the killer?"

"It would be unexpected," Talbot said, "and do not worry, I have hunted in the dark before."

"Well," Clint said, "I may be agreeing to this, but I hope you don't mind if I just go ahead and worry a little."

TWENTY-NINE

Clint sat at the fire, drinking coffee and waiting for everyone to finally settle in for the night. They had agreed that Gerhardt and Mueller would take the first watch while he and Talbot went out into the dark.

"Are you sure that is wise?" Gerhardt asked.

"I'm going along with your buddy Talbot on this, Mr. Gerhardt," Clint said. "I'm assuming he knows what he's doing—unless you tell me different."

"No, no," Gerhardt said, "when it comes to hunting a were—when it comes to hunting, Talbot is an expert."

"All right," Clint said. "I'll take your word for it."

Gerhardt and Mueller came up to the fire now, carrying their rifles.

"We are ready," Gerhardt said.

"Keep the whole camp in sight," Clint said. "But also stay within sight of each other."

Both men nodded. Neither of them looked very enthusiastic. Talbot came walking over. Clint noticed his silver bullet gun was tucked into his belt, and he had his canvas bag slung over his shoulder.

"Are you ready?" he asked Clint.

"Ready as I'll ever be, I guess." Clint dumped the

remnants of his coffee into the fire, wiped the cup off with his fingers, and set it down. "Let's go."

"Good luck."

Talbot looked at his friend intently.

"No matter what you hear, do not leave this camp," he told him. "Do you understand?"

"I understand."

Talbot looked at Mueller, who said, "Yes."

"The lives of these people are in your hands," Talbot said.

Both men nodded their understanding.

As Clint and Talbot got ready to leave the camp, Sarah came running over to them.

"Please be careful, Papa," she said.

"I will," he promised. "You make sure you stay in camp. And near the fire. And stay with Gerhardt."

"I will."

As they started to leave, Sarah grabbed Clint's arm and said, "Be careful."

"I'll watch after him," he promised.

"And yourself," she said, squeezing his arm.

He hesitated, nodded, and followed Frederick Talbot into the darkness.

They were coming for him.

Foolish.

He reached over and wrapped his fingers in fur. Yellow eyes pierced the darkness with a low growl.

They would learn . . .

There was a sliver of a moon, not much light, but that didn't seem to stop Talbot from moving quickly.

Clint tried to follow and step as surely, but still occasionally tripped on a tree root or rock.

"Shhh," Talbot urged.

"Sorry," Clint said. "I can't see as clearly as you obviously can."

"Just step where I step."

"I'm trying."

But at that moment instead of stepping, Talbot stopped. Clint almost walked into him from behind.

"What is it?"

"Listen."

Clint listened, but didn't hear a thing.

"I can hear it breathing," Talbot said. "It knows we're coming for it."

That was bad. They had been hoping to catch the killer watching the camp, perhaps even coming up on it from behind.

"Not good news," Clint said.

"Nevertheless," Talbot said, "it is out here—and that is good news."

Clint thought that remained to be seen.

THIRTY

Clint still could not hear anything—moving *or* breathing—so he had to depend on Talbot, who seemed to have both senses in an eerie quantity.

Talbot started to move again and Clint followed. He found himself wondering if he should have let Talbot make him some silver bullets, after all, then immediately pushed the thought away. If only silver bullets would work, that would make his gun—and his abilities with it—useless. It would also mean that he was out here virtually unarmed. That was not a thought he wanted to carry with him. He had to be ready and alert, and confident in his own ability.

Again, Talbot stopped. Clint turned and looked over his shoulder. He could no longer see the lights of the camp. They were in almost total darkness. Was this really an environment in which Talbot preferred to hunt?

"Frederick—"

"Shhh."

Talbot stopped again. This time, Clint thought he heard it. Was that actually the sound of . . . breathing?

Talbot looked back at Clint.

"We need to separate," he said. "All right?"

"Yes."

"If you hear or see anything, shout," Talbot said. "I will be there with my gun."

"I have my gun."

"I have the silver bullets."

"Ah."

"For my sake," Talbot said, "shout out and I will come."

"You've got it."

"And do not take any chances," Talbot said. "Believe me, you do not know what you are dealing with."

"All right, Frederick," Clint said. "I'll keep that in mind."

"I will go this way," Talbot said, pointing, "and you go that way."

Clint nodded.

Talbot melted into the darkness. Clint wished he could do it that easily.

Back at the fire, Sarah sat nervously rubbing her hands together. Across the fire from her was Gerhardt, standing and staring off into the darkness. She knew he was thinking of his dead son, Carl.

The other man, Mueller, was standing at the other end of the camp, watching. From where they stood, the two men could see each other clearly. That was why Gerhardt was able to watch in horror as something came out of the darkness, grabbed Mueller, and dragged him back into it. Mueller barely had time to scream, and Sarah heard nothing. All she saw was the look of horror on Gerhardt's face.

"Oh, my God!" Gerhardt cried.

"What?" Sarah asked, jumping to her feet. She turned and looked. "Where is Mr. Mueller?"

"He is . . . gone!"

Sarah screamed . . .

Clint heard the scream, knew it came from the camp. He and Talbot had made the wrong decision. They should not have left the camp, not the both of them. One should have remained behind.

Soon after the scream there was a shot.

Clint knew Talbot must have heard both. Was he on his way back to camp? Or was he still out in the darkness?

His own first instinct was to run back to camp, but whatever had happened there was done. There were no more screams or shots. One of each meant that something had happened, probably very quickly, and it was over.

Still, he was caught in a dilemma. Stay out here in the dark hoping to run into the killer and also hoping that nothing serious had happened in camp? Or head back to camp to see what had occurred, while the killer got away?

Talbot heard the scream, knew it was Sarah. But he also knew the worst thing he could do was storm off into the darkness, trying to get back to camp. After the shot he came to the same decision Clint had come to. Whatever had happened was done, over. He just had to hope that the only thing that had happened to his daughter was that she'd been frightened into a scream.

He listened, and heard movement in the brush. He tried to push all thoughts of his daughter aside, so he could concentrate on the moment. Many hunters had been killed simply because they had been distracted. He had been careful for many years not to allow that to happen.

He didn't intend to change that now.

He took his pistol from his belt.

THIRTY-ONE

Clint was moving back toward camp—slowly, not in a panic—when he heard the second shot. It was not from a rifle and not from camp. It was Talbot's gun. He'd fired one of his silver bullets at someone—or something.

Then there were no more gunshots. He could hear the sounds of voices from camp. They were frightened, anxious voices, but he couldn't let that influence his movements.

The sounds in camp came from people who were unsure of what to do. They were not the cries of people being attacked.

Still, he continued to move in the direction of camp. Something had been close enough to it to elicit a scream from Sarah. Maybe something had even entered the camp, and then fled.

Maybe he'd run right into it . . .

Talbot knew he had fired too quickly. He'd been away from hunting too long. His next shot would be more assured, more carefully fired.

He was moving quickly through the dark, chasing the figure he'd fired at. If he could catch the creature before the change, it would be easier to kill. He wouldn't have to worry about the bullet making its way through fur and sinew, just human flesh.

He held the pistol in his hand, uncocked. He didn't want to take a chance on the gun firing before he was ready.

He stopped, and listened.

There.

Moving through the brush. Not running, but moving with purpose. He tried not to think about Sarah, hoped that she was still safe back in camp.

He moved toward the sounds, hoping to intercept the creature before it was ready. He could use all the help he could get, and the element of surprise might swing the balance in his favor.

Now he cocked the hammer back and moved . . .

Clint heard the movement in the brush, and it was coming toward him, from the camp. Whatever it had done, whoever it might have injured or killed, it was now coming toward him.

He took out his gun.

Sarah was remarkably calm, considering it was she who had screamed. But once she'd screamed, Gerhardt said to her, "Stay near the fire," and he ran toward the other end of the camp. She didn't think he could see anything, but he raised his rifle and fired into the dark.

She ran after him, knocked the rifle barrel down before he could fire again.

"You might hit Clint, or my father," she said. "What did you see?"

"I—I—I don't know," he said. "It happened so quickly. First he was there, and then he was not. Something— something took him."

"What was it?"

"I do not know," Gerhardt said. "Something . . . big."

The others came running out of their wagons in response to the scream and the shot.

"Don't tell them," she said quickly.

"W-What?"

"Do not tell anyone what you saw."

"I do not know what I saw."

"Good," she said. "Do not start a panic."

"All right," he said. "All right."

They both turned to face the other members of the train.

It loomed up in front of him, surprising him even though he was prepared. It was a huge shape with fur and teeth and yellow eyes. The creature saw him at the same time and they both reacted. The wolf rose up and roared at him, took a swipe at him with one huge paw. Clint fired his gun twice, was sure he hit the thing, but it turned and ran off.

He chased it, and then realized he had been clawed.

Talbot saw him just a moment before he saw Talbot.

He was large, with long hair, wild eyes, and was totally naked. The look on the poor wretch's face was one of both hunger and suffering. Talbot's heart went out to him, as it always went out to all his prey. He hunted them as much to put them out of their misery as to save himself and his people.

"Stop!" he shouted, but the man-beast came at him and he had no choice.

He fired.

Clint heard the shot. The wolf was moving too fast for him to catch it. And it was leaving a trail behind it that would be easy to follow when the sun came up.

He decided to go back to camp to find out what had happened, and see if Talbot had returned.

THIRTY-TWO

Talbot walked back into camp as people milled about, eyes wide, looking around, wondering what was going on.

"Papa!"

Sarah ran into his arms and he hugged her tightly.

"Are you all right?" he asked.

"You were hardly gone and then—and then—"

"I heard you scream," he said. "I was afraid . . ."

"It wasn't me," she said. "It was Mr. Mueller. He was . . . taken."

"By . . . what?"

"Mr. Gerhardt saw."

They heard someone behind them and turned quickly.

Clint reached camp, saw Talbot and Sarah standing together. As he approached, they turned to look at him.

"You're hurt!" Sarah said right away.

Clint had his hand over his left shoulder, which had been torn by the wolf's claws.

"I'm okay," he insisted. "What happened here?"

"Mueller," Talbot said.

"How?" Clint asked.

"I don't know," the other man said. "I was about to ask Gerhardt."

They walked over to where Gerhardt was standing, looking dazed and pale.

"Sarah," Clint said, "there's a bottle of whiskey in my saddlebags." Bullet had left it with him. "Would you get it, please?"

"Of course."

She ran to get it and brought it back to him. Clint picked up a coffee cup and poured a little into it.

"Drink this!" he said to Gerhardt.

The German did not hesitate. He drank the whiskey down and color immediately returned to his face.

"Okay?" Clint asked.

"Yes, yes," Gerhardt said. "I am all right."

"Now, what happened?" Clint asked.

"It was . . . huge. It came out of the darkness and just . . . took Mueller."

"Did it kill him?" Talbot asked.

"N-Not here in camp," Gerhardt said, "but out there . . ."

"We heard Sarah scream," Clint said, "and then a shot."

"I fired," Gerhardt said, then admitted, "blindly, I am afraid. I don't think I hit it."

"Okay," Clint said, "okay. I don't think it's going to come back into camp tonight. Try and calm these people down and get them back into their wagons."

"Yes."

"Sarah," Talbot said, "help him."

"Yes, Papa."

After Gerhardt and Sarah had left, Clint and Talbot turned to each other and both said at the same time, "I saw it."

"I shot it," Clint said.

"So did I."

"We better have a drink ourselves," Clint suggested. "And a seat."

"Agreed," Talbot said.

They sat by the fire and Clint poured whiskey into two coffee cups.

"You first," he said.

"I saw him," Talbot said. "He was in the form of a man, but his eyes were still those of a beast. I fired once, but I do not know if I hit him. Yet I must have! I do not often miss at that close range."

"Did he leave any blood behind?" Clint asked.

"We will have to go and look when the sun comes up," Talbot said. "I could not tell in the dark, and I wanted to get back to camp to see if Sarah was all right."

"Well," Clint said, leaning forward to speak more softly, "I saw him, too. At least, I saw something. A wolf, I think. But an incredibly large one."

"You saw him in his werewolf form," Talbot said.

"Well, I'm not going to say that," Clint said. "When I saw it, it may have been up on its hind legs."

"Or standing," Talbot said.

"I shot it twice," Clint went on, "and I know I didn't miss. If that wolf is out there, it's injured, or dying. If it's injured, in this country that makes it even more deadly. But here's the thing . . . we fired very close together. How could I have seen it one way, and you another?"

"It must have changed soon after you encountered it," Talbot said. "You did not have silver bullets, but perhaps your shot caused it to change, and then I encountered it."

"I think it's more likely," Clint said, "that we saw two different things."

"You would rather believe there are two killers—man and beast—than believe it is one killer who becomes two beasts."

"I admit," Clint said, "my way is easier for me to believe."

"We will go out in the morning and look for a blood trail," Talbot said.

Sarah came over at that moment, with water and

bandages, and said to Clint, "You must let me treat that wound."

"A good idea," Talbot said, standing. "While she does that, I will talk with Gerhardt. We will set another watch, this time four men."

"How many men do we have?"

"Enough to set two watches for the remainder of the night," Talbot said.

"I can stand watch," Sarah said. "So can some of the other women."

"No," Talbot said, "the men will do it. Just clean Clint's wound."

As Talbot walked away, she said, "He still treats me like a child."

"He treats you like his daughter," Clint said, "but he is right. The men will stand watch. The women should keep themselves and the children safe."

She washed the wound thoroughly, then fashioned a bandage from some torn bits of cloth.

"There," she said, "is that too tight?"

"No," he said, flexing his left arm, "it's fine. Thank you."

She reached out and put her hand on his bare chest.

"Sarah . . ." he said warningly.

She pulled her hand back as if her fingertips had been burned.

"I am sorry," she said. "I will go to my wagon." She stood up, then looked at him and pointed. "It is that one."

He knew which wagon was hers, but he didn't bother pointing that out. He was too busy wondering if that was some sort of invitation. She was a child, but a child on the verge of becoming a woman, and a beautiful one, at that. But she also had her father in camp, a father who was a hunter who would probably kill him if Clint looked at Sarah like she was a young woman.

He pulled his torn shirt back on. He'd change it in the morning for a clean one.

With his shirt buttoned, he poured himself a cup of coffee and waited for Talbot to return and tell him what the watch schedule was. He stared out into the dark, wondering if the killer—or killers—was watching them once again. Or had it—they—gone off to lick whatever wounds they had?

He replayed the events in his mind, wondering if Talbot's rendition could possibly make more sense than his did? One killer who had changed shapes in between encounters?

Two killers traveling together made infinitely more sense to him—and his sanity.

THIRTY-THREE

The killer held his hand to the wound. It was not serious, he knew, but it hurt. He stroked the fur in a soothing gesture.

He watched as the people in the camp composed themselves after the attack. He could have launched another attack, catching them completely by surprise, but the wound had to heal, at least partially.

He knew he was still in control, though.

They were frightened of him. That was half the battle. Only the two hunters were dangerous. They had already proven that, and he had the wound to further prove it.

He was going to have to remove them permanently first before he went after the rest. Once that was done, they would be at his mercy. They would be like a flock of sheep with no master. But he needed a little while—perhaps a day or two—to heal, and then he would be ready.

The next encounter with the two hunters would be their last.

Sarah sat in her wagon, waiting. Would Clint Adams accept her invitation? Or would he be wary of her father? She was willing to take the risk to be with the famous Gunsmith.

She was sorry Carl was dead, of course, but Carl was a boy. The wagon master, Captain Parker, he was just a brute and a lecherous old goat. But Clint Adams, he was a legend. Perhaps he thought of her as a child, a virgin? She would have to convince him otherwise. She had been with men before in her country, but never a man like the Gunsmith.

Her father, and the others, were unfortunately in the way. If Clint did not come to her wagon, she was going to have to try to get him away from camp. He might think her a child, but once she showed him her body—she touched herself as she thought of him—his attitude toward her would change. She was easily as beautiful as her mother had been, maybe even more so. Men in her country were always after her, and the men of America—and the American West— even more. But she had not yet found an American man she would give herself to—until now.

She became drowsy. Perhaps she'd sleep, and he would come and wake her with kisses. Yes, that was what she would do. Sleep . . .

And let her love awaken her.

She reclined, pulled blanket over her, and was fast asleep in seconds.

THIRTY-FOUR

In the morning Clint rolled out from underneath Talbot's wagon, instantly ready.

He looked back and forth, and everything in the camp seemed quiet. Each fire had several women at it, preparing breakfast. The smell of coffee filled the air and made his mouth water.

He walked to one of the fires, and a woman there smiled and handed him a cup of coffee.

"Thank you," he said.

She nodded and went back to her cooking.

Clint walked around the camp, nodding to the people as they came out of their wagons. He also exchanged nods with the four men who had been on watch the last part of the night.

"Anything during the night?" he asked one of them.

"It was all quiet, thank God," one of them said in a German accent.

"Good," Clint said. "Glad to hear it."

He saw Gerhardt stepping down from his wagon, looking not rested at all. He approached the man.

"Gerhardt."

"Mr. Adams," Gerhardt said. "Good morning."

"Are you all right?" Clint asked.

"I did not sleep very well, I am afraid," the German said. "I feel so badly about poor Mueller."

"There was nothing you could have done."

"Really? Perhaps not. Nevertheless, I cannot help feeling guilty."

"I understand," Clint said.

"Will you and Talbot be going out this morning?"

"Yes," Clint said. "Just for a quick look. We want to see if we can find any sign that one of us might have wounded . . . it."

"Then we will not pull out until you come back."

"That's right," Clint said. "We'll come back and roll out with you."

"That is good," Gerhardt said.

"Get yourself some coffee and breakfast," Clint said. "Maybe you'll feel better."

"I doubt it," Gerhardt said, walking away.

Clint turned, walked the other way, and saw Talbot coming toward him, rifle and bag ready.

"Are you ready?" he asked.

"You want some coffee first?"

"No," Talbot said. "Perhaps when we come back. I want to get started."

"Okay." Clint set his cup aside, figuring to pick it up when he returned. "Let's go."

They moved much more quickly through the brush in the daylight. Talbot seemed to know just where they had been the night before.

"I was here when I encountered him," he said, looking around. Clint did the same, and it was actually he who found the blood.

"Here," he said.

Talbot came over, saw the drops of blood Clint had found on a leaf.

"I hit him," Talbot said.

"With your silver bullet."

"Yes."

"All right," Clint said, "I was over here . . ."

It took them a little longer to find the place where Clint had been when he encountered his wolf. And that was what he was thinking of it as, a wolf, no matter how big.

"Here," he said, "this looks familiar. There, see, he broke through that brush."

The branches were bent and torn. They moved in and inspected them.

"Blood," Talbot said, sounding confused.

"And no silver bullets," Clint pointed out.

"I don't understand," Talbot said, "but there's no denying that you hit it."

"We both did."

Talbot touched the blood, rubbed it between his thumb and forefinger.

"We better get back," Clint said.

"Yes," Talbot said, obviously perturbed by this turn of events.

They headed back to camp.

The horses were all hitched up, the campfires extinguished, and the wagons ready. Gerhardt and some of the other men were gathered together, all holding rifles. They looked around when Clint and Talbot reappeared.

"Did you find anything?" Gerhardt asked.

"Blood," Talbot said.

"You hit it?" the German asked.

"Apparently," Clint said, "we both did."

"Then with that many wounds, perhaps it will crawl off and die," Gerhardt said hopefully.

"Perhaps," Talbot said, exchanging a look with Clint. In unspoken agreement, they decided to let the people have hope.

"I'll get my horse," Clint said.

They started walking to Talbot's wagon together. Sarah met them along the way.

"Papa, I don't think Clint should ride with that wound," she said. "I think he should ride in our wagon."

"You are probably right," Talbot said.

"I'm fine," Clint insisted.

"You can still take the lead in the wagon," Talbot said. "Your wound needs to heal."

"Come," Sarah said, grabbing Clint's right arm. "You can still drive the wagon."

Reluctantly, he agreed.

The other wagons waited while Clint drove the Talbot wagon to the front of the column. Talbot mounted his mare.

"I can ride up ahead," he offered.

"Not too far," Clint said. "Just go where I tell you to go. Okay?"

"Agreed."

"Wagons ho!" Clint shouted, and they got under way.

THIRTY-FIVE

Clint wondered if the killer or killers would follow them wherever they went. What if they stayed behind when the train left the state? Whose responsibility would they become then?

He was jostled from his reverie when Sarah put her hands on him from behind.

"Are you all right?" she asked, her voice close to his ear. "How is your shoulder?"

"It's fine," he said, aware of her hands on his neck, his back, then gently touching his shoulder.

"I'll take a look at it again when we stop," she promised him.

"Sarah," Clint said, "I think we should talk."

"Wait."

She climbed out from the back of the wagon to sit next to him on the bench. Sitting that way, they were pressed tightly together, hip to hip.

"All right," she said, "what do you want to talk about?"

"You."

"What about me?" she asked. "Do you like me?"

"Well, of course I like you," he said. "I think you're a lovely girl."

"Thank you."

"But I think you might have the wrong idea about . . ."

"About what?"

"Well . . . us."

"Is there an us?" she asked.

"That's just it," he said. "There can't be."

"Because of my father?"

"Well, that's one good reason," Clint said, "but more than that is your age."

"I am seventeen," she said, "soon to be eighteen."

"Exactly," he said. "I'm a lot older than you."

"I don't care," she said. "I have a woman's needs."

"Well, that might be true," he said, "but I'm not the person to see to them."

"I disagree," she said, closing her hand on his left thigh. "I think you are. I think we are meant to be lovers."

"Sarah—"

"I am sorry," she said, "but that's how I feel."

"No, I mean, here comes your father."

She jerked her hand away from his leg as her father rode up on them.

"It looks clear ahead," Talbot announced.

"Good," Clint said. "We'll take a break in a short while."

"There's a clearing about a mile up ahead, near a water hole."

"Sounds perfect," Clint said. "Lead the way, Frederick."

When they reached the clearing, Clint reined in the team and waved at the others to do the same. He stepped down, mounted Eclipse, and rode back to tell each of the wagons, "We're going to take a break and water the horses. Any of you who want water can step down and get it."

Since quite a few of them took advantage of the stop, they stayed longer than expected.

Clint rode Eclipse to the back of the column and stared out over the expanse of ground they'd left behind. They'd be crossing the border into Iowa soon, their next goal being

Council Bluffs. There they'd have to cross the Missouri River in order to continue. In the old days it took wagon trains many days to cross. In many cases they had to remove the wheels and float the wagons across. There was a lot of personal property at the bottom of the river, along with some bodies. It would not take this train very long, but everyone would have to do what they were told so that they could make it across safely.

But safety had to do with a lot more than just crossing the river. Was there a killer or killers behind them, either following or pursuing?

Clint heard a horse, turned, and saw Talbot ride up alongside him.

"Everyone is filling their barrels," he said. "They want to know if we will be stopping here for the night."

"That'll take some time," Clint said, looking at the sky. "But we still have plenty of daylight. We can travel for another few hours."

"They are worried—you know—about . . ."

"Yes, I know," Clint said. "We'll find a place to camp in the open, so nothing can sneak up on us. That should give everyone the chance to get a good night's sleep."

"And us?"

"What about us?"

"Should we ride back and search?"

"Not in the dark, Frederick," Clint said. "I know you can get around in the dark, but I don't think last night was a huge success, do you?"

"No," Talbot said, "you are probably right."

"We need time to lick our wounds," Clint said, "and I'm not talking about physical wounds."

"I understand," Talbot said. "I will tell them we will be moving on."

"Okay."

Talbot turned and rode away. Clint continued to look behind them.

THIRTY-SIX

They drove for three more hours and then Clint called the column to a halt. They camped as he had said, in the open, picketed their horses, and built their fires. Everyone seemed at ease while they were able to see around them, but as darkness fell, nervousness kicked in. Many felt they might as well have been in the center of a forest for all they could see.

"Let's set the watches by fours again," Clint said. "We'll keep that up all the way."

"All right," Talbot said.

When supper was ready, Clint sat at a fire with Talbot and Sarah. There were two other fires, but he could see that the remaining members of the train had decided to avoid him and the Talbots—or just him. Either they were afraid to be near them, or they were simply putting distance between themselves and his newfound authority.

"Let me ask you something," Clint said to Talbot. He decided to discuss their situation in front of Sarah. She had a right to know what was going on.

"Yes?" Talbot asked.

"I know what a wolf would do," Clint said. "It would follow us as long as we were the only source of food. If, somewhere along the way, he came across another source—maybe easier prey—he'd take it. So I would not expect a wolf to follow us all the way to Council Bluffs. And if it did, we would probably leave it behind when we crossed the river."

"I understand."

"Now tell me about the animals you hunt," Clint said. "Is any of that true?"

Talbot tossed a look Sarah's way.

"Tell him, Papa," she said.

"Yes," Talbot agreed. "In my country this creature would not be pursuing us as a source of nourishment. It would have something else in mind."

"Like what?"

"Either vengeance," Talbot said, "or simple blood lust."

"Vengeance?"

"Against those who hunt their kind," Talbot said.

"And the blood lust?"

Talbot shrugged.

"They simply crave it, from the very first time they taste it."

"Well," Clint said, "we do have animals who, once they've tasted human flesh, can't get enough."

"So if you are asking me if it—they—will follow us to Council Bluffs and beyond, I would say . . . yes."

"That's what I was asking you," Clint said. "Thank you for answering me truthfully."

They ate the rest of their meal in solemn silence.

Clint and Talbot took the first watch along with two of the other men. They saved Gerhardt for the second watch.

Clint took the tail end of the column, while Talbot took the front, near his own wagon. Clint felt safer from Sarah's advances that way. She was a beautiful, healthy young woman and he didn't know how long he'd be able to resist her. He was, after all, only human, and he loved women of all ages, sizes, and colors. But he'd never be able to explain that to her father. So he decided to keep his distance. In the morning he'd tell Talbot to switch places with him and drive his own wagon. Clint was going to be back on horseback, leading the column.

But his secure feeling quickly vanished as Sarah came walking up to him, carrying a cup of coffee. Her hair was down and long, hanging past her shoulders, and her skin was impossibly smooth and pale. In spite of a day of traveling, she smelled fresh.

"I thought you could use this," she said.

"Thank you."

He accepted the cup from her. She folded her arms and stood next to him.

"It's very dark," she said.

"Yes, we could use some moonlight."

She looked up at the sky.

"There are a lot of stars, though."

"Sarah."

"Yes?"

"I seem to remember reading something about were-wolves and the full moon. But we haven't had a full moon for a while."

"You would have to ask my father," she said. "I try not to think of those things. But there are other creatures than just werewolves."

"Vampires, you mean?"

She nodded.

"Yes, but aren't they also only supposed to come out at night?" Clint was trying to remember what he had read specifically. And was it fiction, or fact?

Sarah rubbed her arms, as if cold even though it was a mild night.

"I don't want to talk about this." She turned and walked away.

Clint decided to address these matters with Talbot in the morning.

THIRTY-SEVEN

Thankfully, the night went by uneventfully. Clint had a good night's sleep—well, half a night—and rolled out from beneath the wagon feeling hungry. He could smell both coffee and bacon.

He approached one of the fires, where a fine-looking woman in her forties was cooking.

"Good morning," he said.

She turned and looked at him, startled. She had a pretty face, only lightly lined by the years.

"I'm sorry," he said, "I didn't mean to frighten you."

"I am being silly," she said. "Good morning, Mr. Adams."

"You have me at a disadvantage."

She stared at him, not comprehending what he meant.

"You know my name, but I don't know yours."

"Oh," she said, "I am Bella."

"Bella. Are you traveling with your husband?"

"I was," she said, "but he died soon after the trip started. Fever."

"I'm sorry."

She shrugged and said, "It was many months ago. And it was just like him to force me into this trip, and then to leave me soon after it started."

"You didn't want to come west?"

"I was happy with the life we had," she said, "but he . . . oh, I should not be speaking ill of the dead. Here." She handed him a cup of coffee.

"Thank you," he said, accepting it gratefully. "Are you traveling alone now?"

"I have my son," she said. "He is ten years old. Yes, I know, I look too old to have a ten-year-old. We married late, and had only the one child."

"I would never have said you look too old to have a ten-year-old."

"You are kind. Breakfast will be ready soon."

"Thanks."

She turned her attention back to her task and he turned as Gerhardt, who had been on watch, came walking up to him.

"Quiet?" he asked.

"Too quiet," Gerhardt said. "I admit I jumped at even the smallest sound."

"At least you were alert."

"Yes," Gerhardt said, "perhaps too alert."

"You can never be too alert," Clint told him.

"I suppose not," Gerhardt said. "How long will it take to get to Council Bluffs?"

"About a week," Clint said, "with no trouble."

"What are the chances of that?" he asked.

"We have some wounds to lick," Clint said, "and so does . . . well, it." He was still thinking of two killers, wanting to say "them," but he was traveling with people who believed differently.

"Do you really think so?"

"It won't follow us into Council Bluffs," Clint said. "It's too populated."

He didn't know if that was true, though, since he still wasn't sure what they were dealing with. But he was trying to put Gerhardt at ease.

"Breakfast is ready," Bella announced.

"Get yourself something to eat," Clint said. "We're going to get started soon."

"Yes, all right."

As Gerhardt went to the fire, Talbot came up to Clint and said, "I saw you talking with Bella. She's a fine woman."

"She seems very nice."

"She'd make a good wife for someone."

"I'm not looking for a wife, Frederick," Clint said. "Besides, she's just recently widowed, isn't she?"

"That does not matter," Talbot said. "She needs a man, and her son needs a father."

"Well," Clint said, "I'm afraid I'm not available for either job."

"Too bad."

"Stop trying to be a matchmaker and get yourself some breakfast," Clint said. "I'm going to ride today, so you can go back to driving your own wagon."

"As you wish."

Talbot went to the fire. Clint noticed that breakfast was cooking on the other fires, as well, so he walked over to one of those. No point in asking for a different kind of trouble.

After breakfast they cleaned up, doused the fires, and readied the wagons. Clint felt fairly sure they'd be all right until Council Bluffs. It remained to be seen if they'd be pursued across the river. If they were, then he and Talbot—and the others—would have to come up with some kind of plan of action to deal with the danger. Maybe if they all went out hunting, they'd be able to track it down. The man or the beast. Maybe catching one would be catching the other, even if they were separate entities.

THIRTY-EIGHT

A week later they pulled into Council Bluffs. There had
been no further attacks, although Talbot and Clint remained
as alert as ever. Neither of them really believed that the danger had passed.

"We should be safe in town, shouldn't we?" Clint asked
the night before their arrival. He had not told Talbot that
this was what he had told Gerhardt.

"Not necessarily," Talbot said. "Werewolves—even
vampires—have been known to strike at a large population."

"Really?"

Talbot nodded. "They have their pick, don't they?"

"But you said you think the thing is following the train,"
Clint said.

"That doesn't mean it won't take advantage of a large
population to satisfy its blood lust."

"Well," Clint said, "that would have been too good to be
true anyway."

"Yes."

They stopped their wagons just outside of town and
stepped down.

"We'll need to outfit here for the rest of the trip," Clint
explained. "Also for the crossing."

"How will we do that?" Gerhardt asked. "Is it shallow enough to ride across?"

"That's what I'll have to find out," Clint said. "If not, we'll have to take the wheels off and float them across."

"Float?" another man asked.

"Don't worry," Clint said. "I'll show you how."

"Can we go to town?" Bella asked. "I would like to do some shopping that does not have to do with supplies."

"Yes," Clint said, "you can all go to town if you want. Just stay in a group. If you see a café you want to eat in, go ahead. Get all the comforts out of your system here, because once we cross the river, comforts will be scarce."

The women became excited, as did the children. The men were anxious to find a saloon.

"Don't get too drunk," Clint warned them, "and don't get in trouble with the law. If you end up in jail, I'm not waiting for you to get out. We'll move on."

All of the men nodded their understanding and the entire party made their way into town.

"This must have been very difficult when the wagon trains were longer," Talbot said.

"Just imagine a hundred wagons instead of ten," Clint said.

"That many?"

"And more."

"Will we really leave if one of the men is put in jail?" Talbot asked.

"Probably not," Clint said, "but I want the men to keep that in mind when they're drinking. Where's Sarah?"

"She went into town with the women."

"Good."

"I know my daughter can be headstrong," Talbot said. "Just give her time, Clint."

Clint wasn't sure what Talbot was talking about, but he decided not to pursue it.

"Are you going to town?" Talbot asked.

"I am," Clint said. "I have to find out how the river's running, send a telegram to Effingham, and talk to the local law."

"Why will you talk to the law?"

"I do that whenever I come into a town," Clint said.

"Every time?"

"Pretty much."

"It must be difficult for you."

"Sometimes it is."

"And what about the telegram?"

"I want Ray Bullet to know we made it this far," Clint said. "I also want to know that things are all right back there."

"Why would they not be?" Talbot asked. "The creature at least followed us away from there."

"Maybe it went back," Clint said. "Or maybe there's more than the one we know about."

"I hope not," Talbot said. "They would not be able to deal with it."

"I think they'd figure it out," Clint said.

"I doubt it."

"Well," Clint said, "we'll know soon enough. You going into town?"

"Yes."

"Let's walk together."

"Can we leave the wagons?"

"Sure," Clint said. "There are a few people still here, aren't there?"

"Yes."

"These people are used to having wagons around," Clint said. "They won't bother anything."

In past years, of course, there was lots of thievery when wagons were left unguarded, but just as predators left the boomtowns when the mines dried up, once the wagon trains pretty much stopped coming, the thieves moved on.

"We should be fine," Clint said.

THIRTY-NINE

Council Bluffs had grown even more since Clint's last stop there. Despite the fact that the wagon trains had stopped coming, the town had prospered. He entered what he remembered as a trading post and found himself standing inside a huge general store.

He waited his turn before speaking to the clerk, an older man with a neat gray mustache.

"Wagon train?" the man said to him. "You're about ten years late, ain'tcha?"

"Just some folks who decided to go west as a family," Clint said.

"Well, they're sure welcome to shop here," the man said. He stuck out his hand. "Wade Miller."

"Clint Adams," Clint said, shaking the man's hand.

"What's the Gunsmith doin' working as a wagon master?" Miller asked.

"Just fell into it," Clint said. "I'll tell my people to come in, you can work up one big bill. Okay?"

"However you wanna do it."

"Can you tell me how the river's running?"

"From what I hear, you're gonna have to float 'em," Miller said. "It's runnin' high."

"What happened to Harry Lester?" Clint asked.

"Sold the place to me," Miller said. "Just around when the wagons stopped coming. He didn't see the future, but I did, and I started expanding."

"Good for you," Clint said. "One last question."

"Go ahead."

"Who's the local law?"

"Jasper."

"What jasper?" Clint asked.

"No, that's his name," Miller said. "Sheriff Robert Jasper."

"What's he like?"

"Like a fish outta water," Miller said.

"Wrong man for the job?"

"You'll see."

"Okay, thanks."

"Anytime."

Clint left and headed for the sheriff's office, which he had spotted right across the street.

Clint entered the sheriff's office, which looked and smelled like a newly built structure.

The man behind the desk wore a tie, a jacket, and what looked like a brand-new hat. Beneath the hat was a face that looked as new as the building. If he was thirty yet, it wasn't by much.

"Sheriff Jasper?" Clint asked.

"I am Robert Jasper," the man said, "although I prefer to go by Reverend." He stood up. He was tall and slender, and he wasn't wearing a gun.

"Reverend?"

"That's my true calling," he said.

"But you're the sheriff?"

"The town has no church," he said. "Until I can have one built, this office and badge will have to be my pulpit. What can I do for you, sir?"

Clint understood what the storekeeper had meant. A preacher had no business wearing a badge.

"My name is Clint Adams."

"Yes?"

This was one of the few times Clint had waited for a reaction to his name. He got none.

"I'm here with a train of ten wagons, just a few families heading west."

"Are you the wagon master?"

"I am."

"Well, please tell your members we don't want any trouble while they're here. As long as they know that, I have no trouble with you being here."

"I'm glad to hear that," Clint said. "I just wanted to check in with you."

"I appreciate the thought, sir."

"Sure thing," Clint said. "Have a good day."

He left the office, feeling he had done what he was supposed to do. It wasn't his problem if the town sheriff didn't know who he was.

Clint stopped in at the first saloon he saw.

"Small wagon train just on the outside of town," Hal Wilkins told his friend, Teddy Luther.

"So?"

"So they got women."

"We got women in town," Luther said.

"They got new women," Wilkins said. "And some young ones."

"Young?"

Wilkins nodded.

"How young?"

"Pretty young."

"Well," Luther said, "maybe we should just make 'em feel welcome."

"That's what I was thinkin'."

FORTY

Sarah Talbot stopped in the dress shop with several of the ladies from the train, including Bella. She had seen Bella talking to Clint as they traveled, at mealtimes, and she wanted to know what was going on. So far, she had not been able to lure Clint into her wagon, or even away from the camp. He felt she was too young, but she knew that if she kept working on him, she could convince him otherwise.

She did not need Bella Holstein getting in the way.

"That's nice," she said to Bella, who was looking at a bolt of blue cloth.

"I was thinking of making a dress out of it."

"I'll bet Clint will like it."

"Who?"

"Clint Adams," Sarah said. "Weren't you thinking of him when you decided to make this dress?"

"What an odd thing to say, child," Bella replied. "Whatever are you talking about?"

"Don't you think he's interested in you?" Sarah asked.

"I have given no thought to such a thing," Bella said. "Why would you say that?"

"I have seen the two of you talking . . ."

"I talk to all of the men on the train, girl," Bella said. "But I am a married woman."

"You are a widow."

"Nevertheless," Bella said, "I have given Mr. Adams no more thought than his position as our new wagon master."

"I see," Sarah said. "I am sorry I mentioned it, then."

She moved away and left the older woman to her bolt of blue cloth. She was very happy with the result of her little subterfuge.

Wilkins and Luther knew the women had gone into the dress shop. Where else would a bunch of women go when they first arrived in town?

"Whoa," Luther said, "lookee there."

"See, I told you," Wilkins said. "Ain't she young?"

"She's young and fresh," Luther said, "and pretty."

"And she looks bored," Wilkins said. "Don't she look bored, Teddy?"

"She sure do look bored," Luther said.

"I think we should make her feel welcome in Council Bluffs," Wilkins said, "and let her know there's lots to do."

"I agree."

They stepped off the boardwalk and started across.

Sarah saw the two men crossing the street and knew what was going to happen. She had been through this many times before. It was too bad Clint was not around. She took a quick look up and down the street, did not see any of the men from the wagon. The ladies were all still inside the store.

Maybe she could still turn this to her advantage.

Clint found two of the men from the train in the saloon, standing at the bar. It took him a moment but their names came to him—Leipzig and Heinemann.

They were drinking beer so he joined them, and offered to buy them another round.

"That is very kind," Heinemann said. *"Danke."*

When they all had fresh beers in front of them, Clint asked, "Have you gents been to the general store yet? I've started an account for the train."

"We were going to have one beer," Leipzig said, "and then go over there."

"That is good to know," Heinemann said.

"Tell any of the other men if you see them," Clint said.

"We will tell them."

They sipped their beers. Clint had nothing left to say to them, and they didn't seem to have any desire to talk further with him. As it became awkward, Clint said, "Well, I'm going to have a seat and finish my beer. I'll see you later."

Both men nodded and thanked him again for the second beer.

Clint sat down and sipped his beer. The two men drank down the rest of theirs and quickly left the saloon. While he worked on his beer, no one else from the train came in. The locals paid him little attention. And he doubted he'd run into the local lawman in the saloon, not when the sheriff was actually a reverend.

He finished his beer and stood up. Briefly, he considered a second, then decided against it. He decided to go down to the river and take a look at it himself.

As he stepped out onto the boardwalk, he stopped to look around. He saw none of the men from the train. Neither did he see any of the women, although if he knew women, they were going into as many clothing shops as Council Bluffs had.

He stepped down into the street, crossed over, and headed for the river.

FORTY-ONE

Sarah was nice to the two men.

It was easy. They were young, under thirty, and certainly did not think of her as a child. They wanted to show her the town, so she did not refuse. In fact, she linked her arms through theirs and went along with them very willingly.

"I have been traveling so long with old men," she told them.

"Well, we ain't old," Wilkins said.

"We sure ain't," Luther said.

"You certainly are not," she said. "You are young, strong, handsome men."

Wilkins and Luther exchanged a look and a wink over Sarah's head, which they thought she could not see.

But she did see, and she also saw who was going into the saloon just ahead of them.

"What is that?" she asked.

"What?" Wilkins asked.

"That," she said, pointing.

"Oh," Luther said, "that ain't nothing but an alley that runs along next to the saloon."

"Can we go in there?" she asked.

"There ain't nothin' in there," Wilkins said. "In fact, don't even any light get in there. It's dark as night."

"Well," she said, "that will make it even nicer."

It finally dawned on the two thick young men what she was getting at.

"Oooh," Wilkins said, "the dark alley."

"Yeah," Luther said, "we can go in the alley."

"There's an opening at the other end, too," Luther said. "We could go behind the saloon."

"I think the alley sounds very nice," Sarah said, "don't you?"

"We sure do!"

The three of them crossed the street and entered the alley.

The killer had followed the girl.

First he could smell her, then saw her. When she linked arms with the two men, he wasn't worried. These two were no danger to him.

When she and the two men got to the alley, the killer knew he could get there from the other end. He quickly crossed the street, went around to the back of the building on the other side of the alley from the saloon.

Sarah saw how right the men were. The rooftops of the two buildings hung over the alley, cutting of all light. This was perfect. She only hoped Clint would be able to hear her when she screamed.

"Where are you, little lady?" Wilkins said in a low voice.

"Come on, sweetie," Luther said, "don't hide."

"I am right here," she said, flattening herself against the wall.

She felt one of the men go past her. There were shafts of light from the front and back of the building, but suddenly the light from the rear was blocked out.

Something else had entered the alley.

Sarah was suddenly frightened. This might not have been such a good idea, after all.

"Come on, darlin'," Wilkins said. He reached out and encountered her arm. His hand closed over it.

"Let go!" she said, suddenly panicked and anxious to get out. She could hear the heavy breathing, and feel the hot, fetid breath.

"Come on, honey," Wilkins said, "don't play no games with us."

"Let go! Let go!" she shouted at him. "It's here, don't you see it? Don't you feel it?"

"What are you talkin' about?" Wilkins asked. "Hey, Luther, where are—"

"What the hell—" Luther suddenly said, and then he was screaming.

And Sarah screamed . . .

Clint heard the first and the second screams, even from down the block. He turned quickly, but couldn't see anything. Other people on the street were looking around, and then somebody shouted, "In the alley!"

Clint ran back toward that voice, and yelled, "Which alley?"

"There, next to the saloon."

Clint saw it, and ran toward it just as the man staggered out. At least, he thought it was a man. The figure was covered with blood. One arm was dangling from his shoulder by a string. The eyes staring out from beneath a mask of blood were wide with shock.

And then there was another bloodcurdling scream from inside the alley.

Clint drew his gun and raced into the darkness.

Frederick Talbot heard the third scream as it echoed through the streets. He drew his silver bullet pistol from his belt and started running.

FORTY-TWO

The alley was totally dark. And totally silent, except for the harsh, labored breathing of somebody.

"Sarah?"

After a few seconds she said in a whisper, "Clint? Is that you?"

"Where are you?"

"Here."

He reached his hand out, encountered her hand as she also reached out. She grabbed his hand and pulled him close.

"Are you all right?" he asked.

"Y-Yes," she said, "b-but it was here. The men . . ."

"I saw a man," Clint said, "he's lying in the street."

"There was another man. H-He's still in here."

Clint didn't know if she was referring to the man, or what killed them.

"Stay here," he told her. "Roll yourself up into a small ball and wait. Don't move."

"A-All right."

He moved deeper into the alley.

* * *

Talbot came running up on the scene as people gathered in front of the alley. On the ground was the bloody mass of a man. It wasn't hard to figure out what had killed him.

"Where are they?" Talbot asked.

"In the alley," somebody said.

Another voice said, "Don't go in there."

"There's already a man with a gun in there."

Talbot ignored the crowd and entered the darkness of the alley, hoping that the "man with a gun" was Clint Adams.

Sarah had her arms wrapped around her knees, and her knees drawn up to her chest, making herself as small as she possibly could.

"Clint?" she heard a man's voice call.

"Papa?" she said.

"Sarah," Talbot said. "Where are you?"

"Here, Papa, here," she said. "Right here."

He found her and put his arms around her.

"Are you all right?"

"Yes, Papa, but Clint . . . he's here."

"He can take care of himself," Talbot said. "I am going to get you out of here. Come on."

He pulled her to her feet and walked her out of the alley. She squinted against the sun, then saw the man on the ground surrounded by a crowd. She could not tell from looking at him whether it was Wilkins or Luther.

"Stay with these people," Talbot told her. "I am going back in."

"Be careful, Papa!"

Clint almost tripped over the second man. The toe of his boot struck the body, and he crouched down to feel. His hand came away warm with blood. The man was undoubtedly dead.

Up ahead of him he saw the other end of the alley, with a shaft of sunlight coming through. Cautiously, his gun held out ahead of him, he moved toward it. As he reached the shaft of light, he looked down and saw the tracks. Animal tracks. Wolf tracks.

The wolf had come into town, after all. That was unusual behavior for a wolf. A normal wolf.

He followed the tracks out of the alley, around behind the saloon. There he saw not only wolf tracks, but the footprints of a man.

He heard someone behind him, turned, and saw Talbot step into the light.

"Sarah?" Clint asked.

"She is fine," Talbot said. "I took her out of the alley."

"Good. Look here."

"See," Talbot said. "Two sets of prints."

"The man is wearing boots this time," Clint said.

"Both sets of prints lay over all the others back here," Talbot said.

"So they're together," Clint said. "A man and a wolf?"

"That is what it looks like," Talbot admitted.

"But you still don't buy it, huh?" Clint asked.

"As with you," Talbot said, "I shall keep an open mind."

Well, Clint thought, at least that was something.

"We need to follow these tracks," Talbot said. "This is the first attack in full daylight, and we have time to track them."

"What about Sarah?"

"We will make sure she is safe, and then begin tracking," Talbot said.

"Agreed."

They retraced their steps back through the alley, came out into the sun with the crowd around them. Sarah was there, looking worried. She rushed into Talbot's arms.

"Does someone want to tell me what's going on?" Sheriff Reverend Jasper asked.

FORTY-THREE

The sheriff wouldn't listen to the story on the street. He insisted that Clint, Talbot, and Sarah accompany him to his office.

"Sheriff," Talbot said, "there are tracks behind the saloon that we must follow. I would ask that you have someone safeguard them."

"You are not in a position to make any demands, sir," Jasper said. "No decisions will be made until we have talked in my office."

And so they followed him to the office, where Talbot and Sarah sat and Clint remained standing as the sheriff/reverend sat behind his desk.

"Now, let's start with the young lady. Would you like anything? Water? Tea?"

"No, thank you," she said meekly.

"Then perhaps you can tell me what you were doing in that alley?"

"Th-Those two men," she said, "they forced me into the alley."

"One of them is unrecognizable," Jasper said, "but the other is a man named Wilkins, so I'm inclined to believe the first man is Luther."

"What does that mean?" Talbot asked.

"They were good boys," Jasper said. "They got into trouble, yes, but I cannot see them forcing a young girl into a dark alley."

"Are you calling my daughter a liar?" Talbot asked.

"Not at all," Jasper said, "I'm just telling you what I know of those two boys."

"Men," Talbot said, "they were men, not boys."

"Very well," Jasper said. "Let us agree they were young men." He turned his attention back to Sarah. "What happened after you went into the alley with the two young men?"

"After she was taken into that alley," Talbot insisted.

Jasper simply held up a hand to him to be silent.

"It was dark," she said. "I managed to slip away from them and press myself against the wall. They started looking for me. One of them passed me, but the other one grabbed my arm. Then . . . something happened."

"What, exactly?"

"The first man screamed," she said. "Something was in the alley with us."

"Something?"

"An animal, I think."

"What kind of animal?"

"It was dark," she said. "I could only feel its presence, and feel its breath. It was hot, and it smelled . . . awful."

"Sounds like a wolf," Jasper said, "but why would a wolf come into town?"

"Maybe," Clint said, "he was starving."

"There is a lot of game out there for a wolf," Jasper said. "I can't understand why one would risk coming into a heavily populated town."

"Maybe it was not a wolf," Talbot said.

"Then what?" Jasper asked. "A cat? The question would be the same. Why would a big cat come into town?"

"Perhaps the animal, what it is, has a taste for human flesh," Talbot said.

Jasper looked at Clint.

"Wolves and cats have been known to crave it once they've tasted it," he offered.

"Perhaps," Jasper said. "Miss, I'm glad you weren't injured in the attack."

"Thank you."

"You gentlemen may go," Jasper said. "The crowd told me that neither of you entered that alley until after the screaming started."

Talbot stood up, reached out a hand to help Sarah. Jasper stood, ever the gentleman.

"Miss, if you feel the need to talk to someone about your ordeal—"

"Why would she want to talk to a sheriff?" Talbot asked.

"The sheriff is also the town's religious leader," Clint informed him.

"I am Reverend Jasper," Jasper said. He looked at Sarah again. "If you need to talk, please come to me."

"Thank you," Sarah said.

Clint opened the office door and allowed Sarah and Talbot to precede him.

"Whatever this was," he said, "cat or wolf, what do you intend to do about it?"

"What can I do?" Jasper asked. "I am not a hunter. Do you want me to form a posse to chase an animal?"

"It's been known to happen."

"I will have to give the matter some deep thought, then," Jasper said.

"Well, you do that," Clint said. "Talbot and I will go after it."

"That's your right," Jasper said, "as long as you do not break the law."

"Thanks for your permission," Clint said, and left.

FORTY-FOUR

Clint and Talbot found Gerhardt with some of the other men in a saloon and pulled them out. They told them what had happened.

"Gather up the rest of our people and get them back to the wagons," Clint said. "Take Sarah with you, and watch out for her."

"What are you going to do?" Gerhardt asked.

"We are going to hunt it, and kill it," Talbot said. "We have plenty of daylight left."

"But Papa," Sarah said, "you don't have your kit."

"I have this," he said, touching the pistol in his belt. "That is all I need."

"Please be careful," she said. "Both of you."

"We will," Talbot said. He put his hand on her shoulder, and then gave her a little push toward Gerhardt. "Now go."

"God be with you," Gerhardt said.

Clint and Talbot watched them disperse to go and look for the rest of the group. Sarah remained with Gerhardt.

"Are you ready?" Talbot asked.

"I'm ready," Clint said. "Let's do it this time."

                    * * *

They made their way to the back of the saloon without going
through the dark alley.

"Nobody's been back here since," Clint said, looking at
the tracks. "They still lay over all the others."

"This way," Talbot said.

The tracks continued along the backs of the buildings on
Council Bluff's main street, then veered and headed out of
town to the north.

"It did not go in among the population," Talbot said.

"Well," Clint said, "these are the tracks leading out. We
don't know what direction it came in from."

"That is true," Talbot said.

They followed the tracks up a hill, where they
disappeared—to Clint's eye—into some brush.

"Okay," Clint said, "now it's up to you. I'll just follow
and watch your back."

Talbot took the silver bullet gun from his belt for the first
time and said, "This time we will find it."

Talbot's hunter's eyes picked up the trail and led Clint
into the brush. Clint was very alert as they got farther away
from town and it became eerily quiet. There were no sounds
from birds or any other wild life. That usually meant there
was a predator around.

"It is quiet," Talbot said.

"I noticed."

"I still have two tracks," Talbot said.

"So it is a man with a wolf."

"Or a man with a werewolf."

"Well," Clint said, "since your gun has silver bullets, I
guess we're covered both ways."

They fell silent then, and moved on.

The members of the train came drifting back in, wondering
what was going on. Sarah had built a fire and was sitting by
it, holding a rifle. If her father was right about a werewolf,

the rifle would do her no good, but somehow it made her feel safer. She felt badly for lying about the two dead men, but she couldn't tell the truth about what happened. Certainly not in front of Clint and her father. She was going to have to maintain the integrity of the lie as long as she could.

Gerhardt came over to her, also carrying a rifle.

"We are telling everyone what happened," he told her. "Everyone will be on the alert from now on."

"I hope they're all right," she said.

"Your papa and Clint will kill the beast, if it is possible to kill it."

"Do you think it will come here?" she asked.

Gerhardt's face went pale. His hands tightened on his rifle. "I hope not," he said.

It was starting to get dark.

Their perceived advantage of daylight was fading.

Talbot kept his eyes to the ground. Clint didn't even know if the man noticed that it was dusk.

"Frederick."

"Hmm?"

"It's getting dark."

Talbot looked up.

"So it is."

"What have we got?" Clint asked.

"Wait."

Talbot went down to one knee, moved some of the ground brush so he could see better, then stood up and turned to Clint.

"We have to split up," he said. "The tracks have gone in two separate directions."

"Well," Clint said, "if we have to, we have to. Do you want the man, or the wolf?"

"The man."

"Why?"

"If I am right," Talbot said, "the man can turn into a wolf.

If you are right, then the wolf is just a wolf. You have killed wolves before."

"I have."

"And you do not have silver bullets."

"I don't."

"So . . ."

"I'll take the wolf," Clint said.

FORTY-FIVE

At first Clint had to rely on Talbot's directions on which way
the wolf had gone. But eventually he managed to pick the
animal's tracks up and follow them.

The animal was leading him into an area much denser
with brush and trees. The paw tracks were huge, but Clint
knew he had drawn blood before. He just hoped his pistol
would be large enough to do the job. He would have felt
much more confident with a Sharps rifle.

But a well-placed shot did the job, no matter what the
weapon was.

Talbot followed the man's tracks and quickly realized where
he was going. He was circling, not to go back to town, but
to go to the wagon camp.

He was going after Sarah. That was who he was after in
that alley, not the two men. And perhaps it was who he had
been after this whole time.

The question was why?

The tracks led Clint to some bluffs near the river, which was
running strong. Crossing was going to be rough, but he
couldn't think about that now. The tracks led right to the

base of the bluffs. They didn't turn around, and they didn't run along the base. He had no choice but to go up.

He holstered his gun so he could use both hands.

Talbot could see the lights of the camp up ahead. The boot tracks led directly there. He was about to come out of the brush and enter camp when he thought better of it. If he went into the camp, the killer might change his mind. If he stayed hidden, he might actually get a chance to finish this.

He found a good position in the brush where he had a clear view of the camp. He could see Sarah sitting by the fire, holding a rifle, with Gerhardt nearby.

He settled in to wait.

The killer stared into the camp at the girl. It had been a long time since he'd been near her. Tonight was the night. She would either come with him willingly, or he would take her by force and feed her to the wolf.

He only had to wait for the camp to settle down, go to sleep, except for the men on watch. He could take care of them, and then Sarah would be his.

Caves.

Why were there always caves near water?

The ground was far too hard for tracks. If the wolf had gone into the caves, there was no indication of it. The only way to find out would be to go inside.

It was dark out, but it was even darker inside the caves. Clint had two choices. Go in and look, or wait outside and see if it came out.

Waiting had never been his style. He felt in his pockets until he came across a few lucifer matches. Always liked to carry some in case someone ever offered him a really good cigar. He started looking around for a stout branch to make a torch out of.

* * *

Sarah stared into the fire, unaware of what it was doing to her night vision. Even if something came rushing at her from out of the shadows, it would take a few seconds for her to see it. She'd never even have a chance to fire at it.

"Sarah."

She looked up, squinted.

"Stop staring into the fire like that, girl," Gerhardt said.

"Do you think they are all right, Mr. Gerhardt?" she asked. "Still alive?"

"I am sure they are, girl," Gerhardt said. "I am sure they are."

Talbot stared at his daughter, knowing she was worried about him, but he couldn't bring himself to walk into the camp. Not while the killer was still out there. He had to wait.

Just wait.

Clint fashioned a torch from a thick tree branch with some vines wrapped around the end. It wouldn't burn long, but maybe long enough. He lit a match, held it to the end, and watched it catch and flare up. There was no time to waste. He had to go into the cave.

He drew his gun, held the torch out in front of him, and entered.

FORTY-SIX

Clint moved into the cave, and as soon as he did, he knew he was right. The wolf was inside. He could feel it. He could hear it breathing.

"I can hear you," he said. "I don't know if you're some werewolf creature who came here from Romania, or if you're just some freak of nature from right here in the U.S., but you're not going to kill anybody else."

The creature continued to breathe, and Clint thought he could even feel and smell the animal's hot breath.

"Only one of us is going to leave this cave alive."

His torch began to flicker. He hurried to the mouth of the cave, grabbed some scrub brush from nearby, and took it into the cave. He piled it on the floor and lit it. As it flared up, his torch went out. Now there was a fire on the floor of the cave, between the wolf and the mouth of the cave.

He went out, got some more wood for the fire, and built it up higher. Then he sat down by it, with his gun in his hand.

"This is your only way out," he said aloud, "and you've got to get by me."

Then he thought, I hope this is the only way out.

*   *   *

Under normal circumstances, Frederick Talbot had the
patience of a saint when hunting devils. Tonight he was
growing impatient. The killer had to make a move tonight.
Talbot wanted him dead—he did not want to cross the river
and leave the killer behind to kill again, and he didn't want
to travel anymore while looking over his shoulder.

He left his hiding place and moved closer to camp. His
wagon was still first in line, so he made for it. Without being
seen, he slipped into the back of it. He'd keep watch from
here. His hand was beginning to cramp around his gun, but
he insisted on keeping the weapon at the ready.

From where he was, he could see Sarah sitting at the fire.
Gerhardt was keeping watch, and had walked to the other
end of the train.

Suddenly, a figure stepped out of the dark, into the light
of the fire.

And Talbot knew him!

"Hello, Sarah."

Sarah turned quickly at the sound of her name. No longer
staring into the fire, she saw the man and immediately recognized him.

"Vlad?" she said. "W-What are you doing here? What
are you doing in America?"

The young man walked to the fire. His hair was long,
hanging past his shoulders, and it was matted with dirt and
leaves and twigs. He looked like something that lived in the
woods.

"I came here for you," he said. "I love you."

"But . . . but we left you behind."

"I followed," he said. "I took another boat. I have been
following along."

"Vlad!"

Now it was the young man who turned at the sound of
his name. He saw Talbot standing there with his gun.

"It has been you all along," Talbot said. "You are the killer."

"It is hard to argue with one's nature, Mr. Talbot," Vlad said. "But I will stop killing if Sarah comes with me."

"Sarah will never go with you," Talbot said. He pointed the gun right at Vlad.

"You?" Sarah asked. "It has been you all along?"

Vlad ignored her. His attention was on Talbot.

"Your gun will only kill me if you have silver bullets, Talbot," he said with a grin. "Do you?"

"I do."

"And if you can pull the trigger before I get to you," Vlad said. "Before I change."

With a snarl, Vlad charged toward Talbot, who pulled the trigger twice. The bullets struck the lad, stopping him in his tracks, and then dropping him.

Sarah ran to him, and Talbot walked and looked down. Lying on his back, leaking from two wounds, Vlad Kozlov looked at his hands and said, "I . . . did not . . . change."

And died.

In the cave the wolf suddenly howled. Clint jumped to his feet. It was as if the wolf suddenly felt pain. And then there it was, rising up out of the dark into the light of the fire, coming at him. It was the biggest wolf he'd ever seen, drool dripping from its muzzle as it charged him.

He fired, pulling the trigger six times, all six bullets striking their target. The wolf launched itself in the air at him, but by the time it came down, it was dead. It landed on the fire at his feet, but instead of the large body putting the flames out, the fur caught fire. Clint grabbed one of the great beast's legs and tried to pull it from the flames, but he couldn't budge it. Before long the entire beast was alight, and the cave smelled of burning flesh. Clint backed out of the cave and could only watch as the remarkable animal burned to a crisp.

Who would believe him?

                    *   *   *

By the time Clint entered the camp, the body had been rolled up in a blanket.

"You got him," he said.

"Yes," Talbot said. "And the wolf?"

"Didn't even need a silver bullet," Clint said. "Anybody know how he controlled the wolf?"

"We did not have the chance to ask," Talbot said.

"But you know who he was, right?"

"Yes."

"Well," Clint said, "let's have some coffee. You tell me your story, and I'll tell you mine."

Watch for

STANDOFF IN SANTA FE

382nd novel in the exciting GUNSMITH
series from Jove

Coming in October!

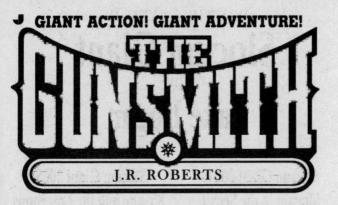

GIANT ACTION! GIANT ADVENTURE!

THE GUNSMITH

J.R. ROBERTS

penguin.com/actionwesterns

M455AS0812

DON'T MISS A YEAR OF

Slocum Giant
by
Jake Logan

penguin.com/actionwesterns

M457AS0812

LONGARM

GIANT-SIZED ADVENTURE FROM AVENGING ANGEL LONGARM.

BY TABOR EVANS

penguin.com/actionwesterns

M456AS0812

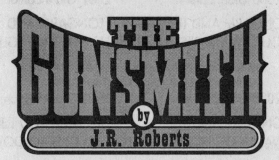
M11G0610